THREE MILLION ACRES OF FLAME

THREE MILLION ACRES OF FLAME

by Valerie Sherrard

A BOARDWALK BOOK
A MEMBER OF THE DUNDURN GROUP
TORONTO

Editor: Barry Jowett   Design: Alison Carr
Proofreader: Marja Appleford   Printer: Webcom

Library and Archives Canada Cataloguing in Publication
Sherrard, Valerie
    Three million acres of flame / Valerie Sherrard.
ISBN 978-1-55002-727-3
1. Fires--New Brunswick--Miramichi River Region--History--Juvenile fiction. 2. Disasters--New Brunswick--Miramichi River Region--History--Juvenile fiction. 3. Miramichi River Region (N.B.)--History--Juvenile fiction. I. Title.

PS8587.H3867T47 2007   jC813'.6   C2007-905458-7

1   2   3   4   5   11   10   09   08   07

Conseil des Arts du Canada Canada Council for the Arts ONTARIO ARTS COUNCIL CONSEIL DES ARTS DE L'ONTARIO

We acknowledge the support of **The Canada Council for the Arts** and the **Ontario Arts Council** for our publishing program. We also acknowledge the financial support of the Government of Canada through the **Book Publishing Industry Development Program** and **The Association for the Export of Canadian Books**, and the Government of Ontario through the **Ontario Book Publishers Tax Credit** program, and the **Ontario Media Development Corporation**.

The author acknowledges, with thanks, the **New Brunswick Arts Board**.

Care has been taken to trace the ownership of copyright material used in this book. The author and the publisher welcome any information enabling them to rectify any references or credits in subsequent editions.

J. Kirk Howard, President

Printed and bound in Canada.
Printed on recycled paper.
www.dundurn.com

Dundurn Press   Gazelle Book Services Limited   Dundurn Press
3 Church Street, Suite 500   White Cross Mills   2250 Military Road
Toronto, Ontario, Canada   High Town, Lancaster, England   Tonawanda, NY
M5E 1M2   LA1 4XS   U.S.A. 14150

For Daniel and Gail Russell

with much love

and

in loving memory of their beautiful daughter

Cynthia Dawn (Blois) Bell

April 23, 1977 – August 1, 2007

"One *thing* have I desired of the Lord,
that I will seek after:
that I may dwell in the house of the Lord
all the days of my life,
to behold the beauty of the Lord and
to inquire in his temple."

Psalm 27:4

CHAPTER ONE

"Give it back! You give it back this very second!" Skye Haverill reached for the spinning top Stewart Drummond had snatched up a few seconds earlier. No matter if he was just teasing her; the top was special to her and he had no business touching it.

"I mean it, Stewart!" Her eyes blazed as she lunged at him. She almost tripped in the process. When he easily avoided her by jumping to one side, the colour rose in her cheeks.

"*My uncle* made that for me! You've no business touching it!" she shouted after several more unsuccessful attempts to retrieve the toy.

"Aw, Skye, don't be like that. After all, we're kin now." Stewart laughed and managed to avoid Skye's hands as she tried a final time to grab the top, reaching behind him first from the left and then the right.

"We are *not* kin," she said, spitting the words out in anger. "Don't ever say that again! There isn't a single drop of blood connecting us."

Stewart looked as though he had just been slapped. He opened his mouth to speak, but it fell closed again before he'd uttered a word. He shrugged and relinquished the top before turning to walk away.

Behind him, Skye felt a twinge of remorse, which she quickly shoved aside. She managed to soothe her conscience by telling herself that, after all, it was true. Just because her father had married Stewart's mother, that didn't mean *they* were tied together. Not the way she was with her real brother, Tavish.

Coincidentally, as Skye was thinking these thoughts, Tavish was walking toward her. It happened that he had been coming around the house, returning from the outhouse, and had witnessed the whole scene.

"When are you going to stop this?" he asked. "It's been more than a year. You've had plenty of time to get used to the fact that Pa is married again. Besides, Hannah's done the best she can, and Stewart surely hasn't given you any cause to treat him like an enemy."

The accusation in his eyes both stung and angered Skye. She lifted her chin as she answered him, her voice shaking with emotion. "It seems you've managed to forget our mother, but I haven't, and I'm not about to."

"It has nothing to do with forgetting our mother," Tavish said with a sigh. He and Skye had argued about this before, but he hadn't thought she'd be so stubborn about it for so long. "Hannah and Stewart are here to stay, Skye. You'd make things easier on yourself if you'd just accept that and try to get along with them."

"I *do* get along ... with Stewart. Most of the time, anyway," Skye protested. That, at least, was true. Her anger over him taking the spinning top was only because of the fact that Uncle William had carved it for her. Uncle William was her favourite relative, and the only one left from her mother's side of the family. He had lived with the Haverills for as long as Skye could remember.

When Skye's mother had died, Uncle William was the one who most understood what she was going through. They had spent many hours talking about Eleanor Haverill, celebrating her life by recalling the light and happy and funny moments, mourning her by their tears or silence when they remembered her final illness and how brave she'd been, even at the end when she was so frail and weak.

So it was natural that Uncle William was the one Skye had turned to after her father announced his intention to remarry.

"It felt exactly as though he'd struck me in the stomach with something hard and cold," she'd sobbed. "How can he even *think* of marrying someone else when Momma hasn't been in the grave a full year!"

Skye had been sure her uncle would sympathize with her. After all, Skye's mother had also been his sister. But his reaction had not been what she'd expected.

"Try to understand that it's been very difficult for your father," Uncle William had said quietly. "A man shouldn't be raising children on his own. And he knows that too much responsibility has fallen to you since your mother died."

"I don't mind! I can do it."

"That may be, although I've seen for myself what a struggle you've had. You've worked hard, but with school and all, you're barely able to keep up with meals and household chores. I know your father feels it's already too much to expect of you, and the heavy load of fall work is still ahead."

That was true. In fact, Skye had wondered how she was going to handle it — making soap and candles, sewing all of their clothing by hand, preserving the winter's food ... the list of extra things that needed to be done for winter went on and on.

"As I said, a man with a family needs a wife," Uncle William had said gently. "It's that simple."

Even so, Skye had been wretchedly unhappy when her father married the widow Hannah Drummond and she and her son, Stewart, moved into the house. This woman was *not* going to replace her mother!

In the beginning, Skye's antagonism toward Hannah extended to Stewart, too, but she soon found it was impossible to maintain that attitude toward her new stepbrother. He was always laughing, teasing, and playing jokes on everyone, and generally making things jolly around the farm. Besides, he worked hard, doing almost as much as Tavish, even though, at fourteen, he was two years younger.

At school, Skye lost no time in telling her closest friends, Mary Taylor and Emily Russell, all about how much she disliked her father's new wife.

"She's always going about with a sour face," she said one day, offering a fine impression of a crabby expression that, in truth, bore no resemblance to Hannah. "And she orders me about as though I were the hired help."

When Mary and Emily commiserated and agreed that it must be horrid to live with such a person, Skye barely felt a twinge of guilt, even though she knew that what she'd said had been unfair.

As the months passed it seemed that her antagonism toward Hannah only worsened. Skye never missed an opportunity to complain and would use the slightest excuse, often ascribing character defects to the woman on the flimsiest of evidence. By the new year, Mary and Emily both felt great sympathy for Skye.

The day that Hannah turned away from her breakfast, claiming she felt unwell, Skye told her friends that her stepmother was now inventing illnesses so she could lie about instead of doing her work.

"Is she lazy, then?" Mary wanted to know.

"Sometimes," Skye claimed, even though she knew perfectly well it wasn't true. Still, she felt justified when, over the next few weeks, Hannah no longer kept up with the work with her former speed and energy.

"She's just getting worse and worse," Skye reported to her friends. "She drags about every morning pretending she can't eat, though you can be sure she sits down to a full plate as soon as no one else is about. It's just an excuse so she can do as little as possible. And Father is so good! He tells her to take a cup of tea and rest if she can. Oh, she must be having a great laugh at how easily he is fooled."

"She's not having a wee one or anything, is she?" Emily said. "My mother gets just as you're describing whenever we're to have a new baby."

Such a possibility had never occurred to Skye. She began to wonder if this could be true, and the question burned in her until she could think of nothing else.

She had to find out. And so, after some weeks of worrying over the idea, she approached the only person she could ask: Hannah.

"I hope you'll soon be feeling better," she said the next time she saw that Hannah was ill.

"Thank you, Skye," Hannah said, surprised at the kind words. "It will pass soon, I'm sure."

"Yes, but you've been unwell for some weeks now," Skye said, forcing herself to sound concerned. "Should you not have the doctor in?"

Hannah looked at her stepdaughter carefully, realizing there was more to Skye's question than what she was asking. She sat her sewing down and patted the bench beside her.

"Come and sit. I guess there's no reason you can't be told," she said in her quiet way.

A few moments later, Skye's fears were confirmed. Hannah was indeed going to have a new baby.

It was the second time in the span of half a year that Skye felt as though her world was being turned upside down.

Chapter Two

The days and months slid by and then it was August. This had long been Skye's favourite month because August was when she had the most freedom. With no school and a lighter load of chores than usual, she spent many hours exploring along the river's edge, or wandering through the cool shade of the woods and drinking in the glorious scents of trees and earth.

It was an in-between time when planting, tending garden, and haying were almost behind them and the huge workload of the fall was still to come. In just a few short weeks, the full harvest would plunge the entire community into a frenzy of work as preparations for winter went into full swing.

But that August day, with the sun warm on her face, Skye thought only of the task she'd chosen: gathering wild berries. She loved the feel of the bright globes, plump and juicy between her fingers, and she loved the sweet smell in the air.

It had rained a little that morning, but by mid afternoon a brisk breeze had blown the rainclouds off and it was once again clear and dry. Skye headed toward a thick cluster of raspberry bushes nestled in among some black spruce and Jack pine trees not far from where the river ran along the south side of their land.

There was time enough to pick a good supply, and Skye sang softly to herself as she neared the bushes. Raspberries were her father's favourite treat and Skye was looking forward to surprising him with a bowl of cream filled with the berries, round and red and bursting with flavour.

Before long, Skye's hands were red and a little sticky. Fearing she would soil her dress, she made her way toward the river to rinse them, but the sound of voices nearby made her stop and stand very still.

"You mustn't ask this of me!" The speaker was a young woman. "I've taken a terrible chance even coming here. Don't make it harder than it has to be."

"Your father will see that he's wrong. He *must*."

Skye's heartbeat quickened as she recognized her uncle's voice, thick and trembling with emotion.

"He can't send you away if you're married," William went on. "Come with me — we'll go straightaway to Reverend Webber's home and ask him to unite us."

"I'd be a widow tomorrow if I did."

"And I'd die gladly for the privilege of being your husband."

Skye felt suddenly faint. The young woman had taken a step back, which brought her into Skye's line of vision. She recognized her at once; it was Charlott Willoughby, the daughter of a wealthy merchant.

"You love me, I know you do," William said, almost harshly. "At least admit that."

"What does it matter if I love you?" asked the girl. "I leave in three days and that's all there is to it."

Sinking down to hide herself in the bushes, Skye tried to make sense of what was taking place only yards away. Uncle William and the daughter of the rich and powerful Desmond Willoughby? It wasn't possible.

"Then I'll come to you!"

"What a splendid idea. I'm sure it will be a simple matter to explain you to my relatives in London and Cheshire," Charlott said. "Anyway, it's not so terrible. I'll be back in a year. Two at the most."

In spite of the casual tone of her words, Charlott began to weep. William stepped forward and pulled her to him, kissing the dark curls that fell over her forehead and telling her over and over that it would be all right.

Feeling like an intruder, Skye moved back as quietly as she could until she was sure she was out of the couple's hearing. Then, forgetting all about the raspberries, she hurried away, her mind in a state of turmoil.

Moments later, Skye was sitting beside a stand of

trees in the upper field, wondering how long Uncle William and Charlott Willoughby had been keeping this secret. In love! It was all so tragically romantic, for it was certain Charlott's father would never consent to his daughter marrying a common woodsman like William English.

The next morning at breakfast, Skye was surprised to see her father in a boiled shirt.* Even though she'd had her weekly bath the night before, she was so preoccupied with William and Charlott that she'd completely forgotten this was Sunday. She had to hurry to get ready to join the others as they piled into the carriage and headed off to church.

It was *so* hard to concentrate on Pastor Webber's sermon that morning! Time after time Skye found her thoughts drifting back to the riverbank and the scene she had witnessed the day before. With Uncle William sitting right there beside her, it was all she could do not to dart looks at him.

How she wished there was some way of telling him what she knew without admitting she'd spied on the pair.

_____

* A clean shirt.

CHAPTER THREE

William was not himself that Tuesday. He spoke sharply to Hannah without cause, pushed away from his plate at the noon meal after barely touching his food, and was generally in ill humour. His behaviour was so out of character that the whole family wondered what might be wrong.

Skye, of course, was the only one who knew the cause of his unusual behaviour, and she felt heavy with sadness for her uncle. How horrible it must be to know that your sweetheart has set sail for England and will be gone for such a long time.

The worst part, she thought, must be the uncertainty Uncle William faced. There was no guarantee that anything would have changed when Charlott returned. And what if she met someone else and fell in love abroad?

A few days later, Skye was dismayed to hear her uncle

announce that he had left his job in the boatyard and was leaving to work in a lumber camp.

"But we'll never see you!" she said.

"Ah, it'll be a good rest for your eyes," he told her. "And I'll be out for a few weeks, now and again."

Skye wondered if this sudden change was so William could escape the familiar places that must remind him of Charlott. Or perhaps it was about money. If he could earn more working in a camp than he could in the boatyard, maybe he could save enough to be a fitting suitor in her father's eyes.

Whatever his reasons, a few days later he was off. Before saying his goodbyes to the family, he spoke privately with Skye.

"I've a small favour to ask of you," he told her. "While I'm away, it may be that a letter arrives for me. Nothing terribly important, mind you, just a note from a friend who's gone off for a bit. As a matter of good manners, I wouldn't want this friend to think I'd just ignored the correspondence. You understand?"

Skye nodded as her uncle struggled to look casual in spite of his heightened colour.

"It would put my mind at rest if I knew someone would attend to it, if such a letter should arrive."

"What would I do, Uncle William?" Skye asked.

"I thought perhaps you might write to the sender at the return address with the message that I'm working at a camp and will answer straightaway when I return."

Skye agreed at once, thrilled that she had been taken into her uncle's confidence, after a fashion. William looked relieved — clearly the matter had been troubling him — and gave her a hug along with a few shillings for postage.

And then, all too soon, he was off, waving cheerily, which, Skye told herself knowingly, was to hide his broken heart.

In the following weeks, Skye found herself too busy to give much further thought to Uncle William's situation. The seemingly endless preparations for a harsh winter took all of the family's time and energy.

Food and heat for the winter took priority, and many hours of work went into both tasks. Root vegetables were harvested, stored in straw, and covered with earth to keep from freezing while grains were threshed, winnowed, and taken to the gristmill to be turned into flour.

Apples from their small orchard were dried and put away, or turned into cider, vinegar, applesauce, and apple butter.

Pigs were slaughtered and cooked and the meat was stored in barrels of brine while the fat was used to make candles and soap for the coming year. Leftover bits of meat were chopped, seasoned, and stuffed into casings made from cleaned intestines — a task Skye didn't care for much, although she greatly enjoyed eating the sausages.

Getting food ready for the animals was almost as much work, but except for corn-husking, which Skye sometimes helped with, that job fell to Tavish and Stewart.

As the family worked together, Skye found it harder and harder to push away any thoughts of the coming baby. Even covered with layers of garments, Hannah's growing belly seemed larger and rounder every day. To Skye, the new baby was a symbol that her mother had been replaced.

She felt no pity for Hannah, even as it became increasingly evident that it was difficult for her stepmother to keep up as the work of the second harvest increased.

"The way she treats me these days, you'd think I was her maid," Skye lamented to Tavish one day.

"It'll be easier for you come the end of the week," he told her. "Father has employed a girl to help out for a bit until the harvest is done."

"Employed someone!" Skye was astonished. "Who?"

"Abby Gunn," he said. "She's the girl who works for the Carpenters." Tavish's face reddened when he said Abby's name, but Skye missed it, being too preoccupied with her own thoughts.

"I remember her from school a few years ago. Why, she's not much older than me!" Skye said indignantly. "She must be about sixteen — like you, Tavish."

Tavish was quite aware of Abby's age, but he shrugged

as though it was of no consequence to him. In truth, the thought of having her in his home for the next while was the most pleasant thing he could imagine.

"I wonder that the Carpenters can spare her," Skye said.

"They haven't so much extra to do at harvest time," Tavish reminded. "I expect their store is busier, but it's not as though they have to bring in crops and all. Anything they need — meat, vegetables, flour, and the like — they can take in trades for store goods."

"I suppose that's true," Skye said. She couldn't help but think how wonderful it must be to have a store like the Carpenters'. It was always exciting to go there, even if they were only buying everyday things like tea, molasses, oats, or the enormous barrel of salt they needed every year. If there was an extra farthing or halfpenny, Skye might be treated to a stick of candy or a ribbon for her hair. Tavish poked fun at her for being excited about such treats, but she thought him most peculiar for wasting his time looking at things like axe heads and saws and even lead balls for his musket when they went to the store.

No matter why they were there, Skye loved to look at the new bolts of cotton and to smell the spices. She thought it must be exciting for Abby, working for the Carpenter family. Even if her job were not in the store itself, she would surely have ample opportunity to go there.

"I don't suppose she'll be thrilled to come here," Skye said, thinking aloud, but Tavish seemed to have drifted off with his own private thoughts, and he didn't answer.

Abby arrived on schedule that Saturday afternoon on the tenth of September.

"I've come to help Mrs. Haverill for a bit," she announced when Skye opened the door to find her carrying a small bundle that held the clothes she'd brought.

Skye led her inside and showed her where she could put her things. A new straw tick* had been made in preparation for Abby's arrival, and it was arranged in the loft beside Skye's.

They returned to the kitchen and joined Hannah, who was busily carding† wool. Working along with her, Skye and Abby spun the slivers of wool onto drop spindles until Logan and the boys came clomping in for their supper. Then, laying their work aside, the two girls set the table and filled the plates with the thick venison stew that had been simmering in the fireplace.

Abby had taken a few moments to add dumplings to the pot a bit earlier and she worried aloud that they hadn't turned out as well as she'd hoped.

"Oh, but they're grand!" Tavish assured her. "Best

---

* Mattress.

† Untangling wool by combing it with wire-studded, wooden paddles.

ever." To prove it, he hurried over to the pot and added more to his plate as soon as he'd finished with the first helping.

Skye was inclined to agree with Abby. The dumplings were heavy and could have used more salt. She thought it odd that her brother found them delicious.

Not many days passed before Skye realized the reason for her brother's enthusiasm with Abby's cooking — and, for that matter, anything else that Abby did. In fact, it was clear to everyone in the house that Tavish was smitten with the girl.

Everyone, that is, except Abby. If she was aware of Tavish's infatuation with her, she didn't let on. Skye was curious about what Abby thought of Tavish, but could think of no way to bring the subject up without giving her brother away.

In any case, with preparations for winter upon them, there was little time for speculation along those lines. Hannah and the girls worked from morning until night, and for the first time Hannah admitted to herself that she was glad her husband had hired Abby to help. The girl was a good worker and had taken over many of the more arduous fall tasks that would have fallen to Hannah.

The crops this year were not as bountiful as they had been for other harvests, but that was to be expected, considering how dry the summer had been. Hannah noticed that they received more calls from the nearby Mi'kmaq women than was usual and realized that they, too, had been affected by the unusually hot weather and lack of rain.

The Mi'kmaq women came with tanned deerskins and finely woven baskets and berries and fish, hoping to trade for tools and flour and other items of the settlers' goods. Hannah traded some tea and oats for a large, sturdy basket, which she saw would make a suitable bed for the new baby when it arrived. It was the only exchange she made that fall, although she was tempted by beautifully tanned skins several times.

Skye wished she had something to offer for an article of beaded clothing that caught her eye, but she had nothing to trade. Later, she and Abby discovered that they had both longed for the same garment! As they talked of the other things the Mi'kmaq ladies had brought, Skye suddenly found herself talking about her mother.

"When she first came to Canada, she was terrified of the Indians," she said. "Imagine that!"

"But why? They're so gentle and gracious," Abby said, astonished.

"She didn't know that. And she'd heard some peculiar stories about them."

"Mr. Carpenter told me that if it wasn't for things they learned from the Indians, a lot of settlers wouldn't have survived the hardships here," Abby said. "It's strange that people would judge them before they even got to know them."

Skye nodded, but Abby's comment had brought

Uncle William to mind and she found her thoughts drifting to him. If only Mr. Willoughby knew him, he'd be happy to have Charlott marry William.

CHAPTER FOUR

Friday, October 7, 1825, began like any other day. Families rose and started into their normal routines without a great deal of thought for the weather, which was unusually hot and dry for that time of year. It hadn't rained for some weeks and the leaves, already shifting into their fall colours, were brittle and crumbled easily.

Skye's first thought when she slipped outside to go to the outhouse that morning was that there was a heavy mist from the river. In the pre-dawn air it looked like a low-hanging fog, but the smell that hit Skye's nose quickly contradicted that idea. Instead, the acrid odour of smoke told her that the grey cloud was from burning wood.

"You put me in mind of a rabbit," Stewart said as he came up behind her. Skye started and turned to him, more curious about his comment than angry because he'd made her jump.

"Sniffing the air that way," he explained. He put his nose up and demonstrated with a rapid series of short sniffs.

"It's smoky," Skye said with a frown.

"Ah, that's nothing. Just some trees burning a ways off. No different than any of the other fires lately."

"I wasn't worried about that," Skye said. In the last weeks, there had been a number of small blazes not too far off, but she knew that good, wide clearings stood between the town and the surrounding forests, protecting the settled area from spreading fire. "It's just that we've wash to do today. I don't want the clean clothes to smell of smoke, now, do I?"

"Well, the air will clear before long," he said. "After all, there's a good breeze."

Skye was pleased to see that he was right. By daybreak the haze had been swept along, though it hung in a purple cloud on the far side of the river. She and Abby hauled water to the cauldron, added two cups of the soap they'd cooked in the very same pot a few weeks before, and began washing the clothes.

Before long, their hands were red and sore. The lye in the soap, along with the rough scrubbing-board surfaces, made the task particularly unpleasant. Even worse, the air was hot and suffocating. Their early chatter stopped as they laboured to breathe while they worked.

Suddenly, Abby let out a little scream, dropping the

shirt she'd been cleaning. Skye looked up, startled, and saw that a crow was lying at the other girl's feet.

"It just fell from the sky," Abby said, taking a step backward.

"Is it dead?" Skye asked, but the answer was obvious. The crow was still, its black eyes staring ahead sightlessly. The girls inspected the bird and found that its wings were charred.

"Must have been escaping one of the nearby fires," Skye said. She nudged it with her foot, but there was no response. "I'll ask Tavish to get rid of it."

"Tavish and Stewart are gone to your uncle's house until tomorrow, remember?" Abby said. "They're helping with an outbuilding and staying at his house for the night."

Skye felt a tug of annoyance that she hadn't known the boys' plans, until she remembered Hannah mentioning something to her the previous evening. She'd been preoccupied with thoughts of Uncle William and Charlott and hadn't really listened to what her stepmother was saying.

Just then, a thunderous crack rang out, and this time both girls started.

"I've been half-fooled into thinking a storm is coming more than once since yesterday," Skye admitted with a rueful smile. "I'll be glad when it rains and the forests quiet down. Who'd think snapping trees could be so noisy?"

"They're terribly loud," Abby agreed, turning back to the steaming cauldron. "All that breaking and crashing ... it sounds like a war being fought."

But there was no war, and the girls worked without worrying about the horrible sounds of explosions in the woods. Neither did they pay much mind to the spires of smoke that snaked up here and there in the distance. After all, fire never crossed the cleared lands.

Others in the communities of Newcastle, Douglastown, and Chatham were far more concerned than Skye or Abby, but their fears were for the wood — and the trades that occupied so many of the area's inhabitants. Lumber and shipbuilding were the main sources of income for many families, and any serious depletion of the forests could threaten their very livelihoods.

As the day wore on, the noises from the woods crept closer. Crackling, crashing, and moaning sounds created a background for the sharp explosions, which were now nearly constant. Adding their voices to this, several of the town's men rode through, shouting warnings of great peril to come, but their cries failed to raise any real alarm.

After all, the inhabitants reassured themselves, there was no danger to the town.

In the late afternoon, Hannah paused near the girls on her way back to the house from the necessary.[*]

---

* Outhouse, or outdoor toilet.

Although nightfall was hours away, the sky had turned black as an immense pillar of smoke rose in the air northwest of Newcastle. A strange feeling of foreboding came over Hannah and she wished that the boys had not gone off for the day. She tried to pray, but the words died half-formed on her lips.

Standing very still, hands clenching at her apron, Hannah watched as the enormous cloud of smoke slowly broke up, pushed apart by a light, northerly wind, and finally dispersed into fading mists.

"Hannah?"

Turning, she saw Abby looking at her anxiously. "Did you want to take your supper now?" the girl asked. "Mr. Haverill said not to wait for him as he'd be late."

"No, thank you, Abby," Hannah said. "I was just watching the sky." She shook her head slightly, as though admitting to some act of folly, and went back into the house.

As hot as it was outside, the house was even more oppressive with the fireplace going steadily and no breeze to help. Hannah took a few bites of the fish soup she'd prepared earlier, but was unable to eat more. She sat staring at the table, too overcome with fatigue to move.

"Are you all right, ma'am?" Abby asked.

"Yes, fine." With a great force of will, Hannah lifted her head and smiled. "It's just that the air is so close and hot. I feel as though I'm breathing through a heavy blanket."

"It's hard on *all* of us," Skye said.

"They say it's the fires all about, keeping it so hot and making it so hard to breathe," Abby said. "What we need is a good rain."

The three fell silent, overcome with indolence, and when the meal was finished they did their chores sluggishly and sat outside, hoping to take advantage of any breeze that might spring up. Abby remarked once more how good it would be to see it rain, but there was little else said. Aside from the lethargy that had overtaken them, their throats were too parched for conversation.

Darkness fell too soon and the three retreated back into the house and prepared for bed, carefully folding and laying aside their dresses and pulling on nightgowns. None of them slept. Hannah lay waiting for the sound of Logan's arrival home, at which time she would get up, light the candle she'd put by his bowl, and dish up his supper. Skye and Abby tried to shut out the dreadful sounds of the woods burning a short distance away.

And then, a strange pause came as silence fell. Skye felt her heart quicken with an unexplained fear at the sudden calm.

"It's stopped," Abby whispered. "Just like that!"

"The sound of death," Skye said in return, her voice hollow. "It's like the forests have died."

Abby laughed uneasily, trying to make light of the remark. "You've quite the imagination," she said. "Anyway, the quiet is an improvement, wouldn't you say?"

"Perhaps."

But there was no more discussion on that point, because just then a terrible and mighty roar filled the air. Skye and Abby sat bolt upright on their mattresses, hearts pounding.

Downstairs, Hannah had risen unsteadily to her feet at the sound. Hurrying to the door, she gasped in horror at the sight that met her eyes. The wind had risen with incredible speed and fury. As far as the eye could see, sheets of flames rose in the air, lifted and carried along by enormous gusts.

In a flash, the unthinkable had happened. The fire had crossed the clearings and was descending in airborne waves upon the town.

"Girls!" Hannah shrieked, rushing back into the house. "Come quickly!"

Skye and Abby obeyed at once, propelled in part by their own fear. As they reached Hannah's side in the doorway, they could scarcely take in the sight before them.

A great, rolling wall of fire was moving with relentless speed, swallowing up everything in its path.

"The river!" Hannah cried. "Hurry."

Abby moved at once, fleeing from the advancing inferno, but Skye seemed frozen in place. Hannah screamed her name several times, but the girl stood as though in a trance. It wasn't until Hannah delivered a sharp slap to her cheek that the spell was broken and Skye's feet obeyed.

Skye and Hannah raced through the lower fields and bushes, hearts pounding with fear. Hannah stumbled over a rock; Skye grabbed her arm and roughly pulled her back upright. Behind them, they could feel the heat of the flames and hear the crashes of whole trees being hurled burning into their town.

As swiftly as they moved, it felt as though their progress was maddeningly slow, as though they would never reach the river before the flames engulfed them.

For miles around, animals and people joined in a frantic race for the safety of the mighty Miramichi River. Men, women, and children, cows and horses, moose and bears, ran side by side with one purpose in mind: to plunge themselves into the water.

CHAPTER FIVE

A surge of relief ran through Skye as they reached the river and lunged into the water. At first, she and Hannah waded out only a few feet, but they were forced further by the burning debris blowing in the air around them.

Everywhere they looked, the faces around them were staring back toward Newcastle. Skye thought that was only natural as she and Hannah also turned to face their town. Who would do otherwise? Their homes, outbuildings, livestock, provisions for the winter, and indeed, everything on which their survival depended, lay behind them.

Newcastle! Their beautiful town, nestled snugly between the river and the nearby forests, had been a thriving community. Its inhabitants had rejoiced in the growing prosperity and had looked with satisfaction on the well-stocked warehouses on land and, on water, the fleet loaded with the lumber that was the mainstay of their existence.

But now, the sight that met them bore no resemblance to their peaceful, thriving town. In the space of only minutes their happy community had been turned into a scene so horrifying they could barely take it in.

As far as the eye could see, a moving wall of flame rolled and boiled, burying everything in its path. The wind howled and roared, filling the air with pieces of flaming buildings, branches, and even whole trees that had been ripped from the earth by its mighty force. Chunks of burning wreckage, large and small, were thrown about as easily as a child might toss a pair of jacks.

Almost at once prayers began to rise from the land and from the water in Newcastle, Douglastown, and every settled area that found itself in the path of the great fire. Prayers and wails and pleas poured forth. They begged God for rain, for mercy, for light.

But most of all, they prayed for deliverance.

There were those whose shouts proclaimed that this was the great judgement, the time of tribulation foretold in scripture, and Skye thought it quite possible they were right. In the fear, panic, and desolation of that dreadful night, prayers of repentance and conversion joined those that cried out to God for rescue.

As she took in the terrible scenes around her, Skye noticed Hannah's lips moving silently as they stood in the water. She wondered bitterly whether her petition included Logan and Tavish, or only Stewart. This unfair thought was born of shame, for she had almost forgotten to ask deliverance for her stepbrother when she herself had bowed her head a moment earlier.

It was this omission that nudged her memory further, and she strained to see if she could find any sign of Abby in the scattered assembly of man and beast now taking refuge in the river.

It seemed that Hannah had thought of the girl in the same instance, for she called out Abby's name several times. Her effort was as useless in the din as the many other voices that rang out calling for loved ones — parent for child, child for parent, and every other combination of kin and friend.

The noise was frightful! Worst of all were the tortured screams and cries — almost lost in the deafening roar of the fire — of men, women, and children who had not made it to safety. Along with the thunderous splitting and crashing of trees and buildings came the groans and bellows of the many animals that had not managed to escape the fire.

Other animals, both domestic and wild, had reached the river before the flames overtook them, and it was an odd sight to find them gathered like frightened comrades. Skye stared, barely comprehending what she was looking at, when she saw a bear standing peacefully in the midst of a group of cows. The strange collection of animals added a cacophony of sounds to the commotion.

Heat and flames were everywhere and the very river itself seemed in danger of igniting as the water near the edge grew ever hotter, foaming madly, joining its own voice to the raging inferno.

Skye tried to block out the sights and sounds, but there was no way to escape the assault on her senses. Her eyes stung, her throat burned, and she laboured for oxygen through the thick cloud of smoke and ash that surrounded her.

A few yards away, a young mother holding a baby to her bosom screamed as a burning ember struck the child and ignited its nightdress. The mother ducked into the water to extinguish the flame and emerged with the baby wailing in pain.

It was in this nightmare of chaos and horror that Hannah felt the first contraction: a sudden, wrenching pain that told her labour had begun. Fear paralysed her for a moment, but the instinct to protect her child soon conquered it.

"Come," she said, taking Skye's hand when she realized she must act as quickly as possible. She tugged her stepdaughter toward a larger group gathered nearby, hoping that someone there could help.

When they reached the others, Hannah asked several of the ladies if there might be a midwife among them. Her question was passed from person to person until one gentleman, a Mr. Davidson, heard of her plight and hastened to help.

"Come with me, madam," he hollered above the bedlam when he reached her side. "There are a number of rafts here. We will entreat someone to yield place enough for you."

As Hannah followed the good man, he asked those they passed if any could help with the birthing of a newborn. While no midwife could be found, a matronly woman offered to help as much as she was able, and joined the little group.

They reached the first raft shortly, but it held a young mother with three children, all four suffering with fever, and several others who had received burns and other injuries.

The second raft was even less hopeful, and the third was more submerged than floating, so overloaded was it with the wounded and ill.

But then they came to the fourth, and Davidson was outraged to discover an able-bodied man among its passengers.

"What manner of man are you?" he demanded, taking hold of the cowering fellow's arm. "You'll yield your cowardly perch to this woman at once."

"But I can't swim!" the man cried, clinging to the rough wood.

"Swim or not, he can steal a'right," came an old woman's voice nearby. "More beast than man, he is! This black-hearted monster robbed me — his own mother-in-law — of fifty pounds ... thinking, no doubt, that I'd not make it to safety."

"Swim or sink, you devil, it's all the same to me," roared Davidson. With that, he gave a mighty pull, dislodging the whimpering scoundrel and flinging him into the water. The man thrashed about and it seemed likely he would indeed drown until Davidson grasped his hair and yanked him upright.

"You'll not drown in water that comes to your chest unless you're a bigger fool than I've yet seen," he told the sputtering fellow. "Anyway, better to see you tried for your crime than escape so easily as that."

Then, paying no further attention to the coward, he helped Hannah onto the raft. The contractions were coming steadily and with surprising speed by then, brought on by the shock and upheaval of the last hours. Hannah let herself sink into the pain, almost welcoming the way it drew her into it — and away from the horror around her.

Skye stood a short distance away, watching her step-mother and hearing her cries without really taking any of it in. A heavy numbness had crept into her and she felt as though something had frozen her very heart.

And then she heard her name! Turning toward the joyful cry she saw her father pushing toward her, his face twisted with emotion.

"Thanks be to God!" he said as he reached her. He threw his arms around her and drew her to him. Something broke inside her. Tears came, along with great shuddering sobs, and it was only with difficulty that she was able to compose herself enough to answer his questions about Hannah.

When he learned of his wife's situation, Logan hastened to her side, taking Skye with him. It seemed that, even in the throes of a contraction, Hannah's face softened just a little with relief.

"The boys?" she gasped when she could speak again. "They are with you?"

"I was well on my way home when the fire struck," he told her, careful to keep his voice even. "The boys had stayed behind with Collin, as planned earlier. But don't worry, we'll find them as soon as we're able to return to land."

Shooed off then by the woman tending to Hannah, Logan and Skye moved back to the group standing in the water. Some had made off for the far shore, determined to swim across the river where it seemed the fire had failed to take hold. Most, however, remained behind and waited. Man and beast, they waited together.

On and on the wind and fire continued their deafening ruin. And yet, during that night of destruction and death, another sound was heard. That sound — rising like a promise — was the bleating cries of newborn babies.* Hannah's child was but one of these — a

* At least thirteen babies were born in the affected areas during the Great Fire of Miramichi.

41

daughter, born near dawn, and swaddled in a wet scarf offered by one of the ladies.

The child was small, but her lusty cry suggested she was healthy enough. Hannah remained on the raft with her new daughter while Logan and Skye returned and stood at her side in the water as the fire blazed on.

The minutes of the night crept by while the towns-people converged, fighting hunger and exhaustion. Through the longest hours of their lives, they waited. And as they waited, they wept and prayed. And then, at last, their prayers were answered. The storm clouds broke and rain fell, pouring down in torrents on the burning communities.

Even so, the fire was not easily beaten and it was not until the next day that they were able to emerge from the river, wet, weary, and starving.

They moved slowly, dragging themselves onto the black banks, wading through soot and ash to their knees. Numb with shock and fatigue, they could not yet absorb the fact that their world had been wiped out in the space of a single night.

It would be days, weeks, even months before their losses were defined and measured. Until then, they felt no more than the weight of each moment as it crept by.

CHAPTER SIX

Everywhere, hacking coughs and laboured breathing could be heard, together with the sizzling, snapping sounds of the dying fire. Skye choked as she breathed in soot and the acrid odour that was impossible to escape. The overpowering smells of burnt wood and flesh sickened her and, like many others, she found herself retching, although her stomach had nothing to yield.

The group's movement was difficult as the survivors plodded through the sludge at the river's edge, stumbling and dragging themselves through the sea of soot and grime. Still, it was the air that was the worst. It almost seemed as though it was as thick as the mire through which they made their way. Indeed, so immense were the bodies of smoke that hovered around them that it was impossible to see ahead more than a few yards at a time.

Skye, like the others, kept her head low and her

hand over her mouth in an effort to filter the smoke and ash, but it was of no use. It felt as though a heavy weight had been placed on her chest and every breath was an effort.

Beside her, Hannah held a thin cloth close to her newborn daughter's face as she plodded along. Her own struggle to breathe was compounded by the weakness she felt after the forceful labour and delivery. Hannah had nursed the babe several times since her arrival, but since she herself had had nothing to eat or drink for more than twenty-four hours, her condition was increasingly frail.

Several times she faltered, began to sink to her knees, and had to be caught up by her husband. Skye watched her father as he helped his wife back to her feet. For the first time, she felt something other than resentment toward this woman who had come along and taken her mother's place.

Images from the night before flashed through Skye's head. Hannah's face, white with fear, clasping her hand, trying fruitlessly to tug her toward the door. She heard the echo of her stepmother's screams. "Skye! Skye!" It was as though Skye's ability to move had been swallowed by shock and fear. The sharp sting of the slap, when it came, had been enough to do the job, jolting her into action, prompting her to run with the others toward the river.

I'd be dead, Skye thought, if it hadn't been for her.

She went no further with the musing, unable to think much past the immediate moment. Drained of energy as she was, it seemed that thirst, hunger, and cold were enough to contend with.

It took all of her strength to tread through the soot and ashes that lay everywhere. In many places it was several feet deep, laying on the ground like heavy black snow.

"Better we'd been burned or drowned," came a bitter cry from nearby. "T'would have been a happier fate than what lies ahead for us, sorry lot that we are."

"The Good Lord has seen fit to spare our lives." Reverend Webber spoke with dignity even though his voice was heavy with grief. "We must be thankful for His mercy, and lean on Him for strength and comfort for all we have lost."

"So you say," someone scoffed. "But what have *you* lost, Reverend?"

"We have all suffered loss," Pastor Webber answered quietly. "Last night, my wife Elizabet, whom most of you know, and our infant, little Peter, perished in the river we have just taken ourselves from."

Skye felt her eyes widen in shock as the meaning of his words sank in. At her side, Hannah began to weep and Skye heard her moan and whisper, "Not dear Elizabet and the wee one. It mustn't be."

But it was. After reaching the water with his family the night before, the pastor had swum out to see if there might be a place for Elizabet and the children on one of the small boats floating a ways off. Two of their offspring had been sick with the fever that had swept through the community in recent weeks and he feared any prolonged time in the water would weaken them further.

But when he made his way back to them, Elizabet and Peter, whom she'd been holding in her arms, were gone. And so it was that, even as he offered words of faith and comfort to those around him, Reverend Webber's heart was filled with grief.

With heavy heart, he led his three remaining children, along with the gathered group, toward the town where their homes had all been.

There was little in the sad journey that gave the weary group hope of finding anything other than the desolation they had already encountered. Oh, now and then a cry of relief would go up when a building was found standing, but most of the families' fears were realized as they reached their properties and discovered that they had been entirely destroyed by the fire.

Where their homes had once stood, all that was left to mark their existence was mouldering heaps of debris. Gone too were the courthouse, the barracks, the gaol,* the church, and almost every merchant building.

Skye watched in horror as an elderly woman fell to the ground and embraced a charred body. She recoiled

---

* Jail.

as the woman let out an unearthly wail.

Two children of around eight and nine called plaintively for their mother, as though she might emerge from the wreckage at any moment, smiling and well. When they'd all heard it over and over someone cried, "For pity's sake, silence those children. I cannot stand to hear it again!"

Skye focused her attention on the destroyed buildings, and would not look at the bodies that lay here and there.

In most cases, only the blackened chimneys re-
ained, jutting up like gravestones in silhouette, as
ch they had erected themselves in the night to mark
ots where the dead had fallen — overcome by
me, a few paralysed by fear.

of all was the death. It lay everywhere: the
mains of man and animal. Many of those who
een caught in the flames were charred beyond rec-
nition, while others who had drowned and washed up
on the shore had begun to bloat and swell.

Some had split, spilling forth bowels, revealing half-burnt flesh. Others' heads had been so badly burned that the brains were exposed. The terrible sights made a few of the women faint in shock and horror.

"We shall *all* perish."

Skye looked to her right and saw that it was Lavinia MacFarlane who had spoken. She walked stiffly, eyes straight ahead, each hand holding onto one of her four-year-old twin boys. Her husband had been injured in an accident at the lumberyard that summer and since then the couple had depended on help from the townsfolk just to survive. But now, no one had anything to give.

Skye wondered if Lavinia's words might well be prophetic.

CHAPTER SEVEN

Old Mr. Fraser was the first, on reaching what was left of his house, to dig into the root cellar to see if any of the provisions stored there had survived. After scooping away the burnt top layer, he discovered that the vegetables underneath had roasted in the heat and were quite edible.

It was good news for the moment, for it satisfied the sufferers' pressing hunger, but at the same time it was another cruel blow against them for the coming winter. What wasn't eaten quickly would spoil and rot. There would be nothing saved for the months ahead.

Over the next few days, those who remained on the north side of the river survived primarily on roasted potatoes and — until it turned foul — fish, for thousands of salmon, bass, and trout lay at the shore's edge, dead from bruising and suffocation, and cooked by the heat of the fire.

Many of those who had been laid destitute sought refuge on the other side of the river. Clustered in wretched groups, they waited for boats to take them across the water to the town of Chatham. Those with injuries were sent first but even so, several died waiting for help to arrive.

It was Sunday afternoon when the Haverills managed to obtain crossing on a small boat belonging to a Chatham resident named Elias who, along with his brother Charles, was making his third trip that day to ferry passengers across the Miramichi River. They climbed into the craft with several other people and huddled together in an effort to keep warm.

"Thankfully, the buildings in Chatham were not much harmed by the fire," Eli told them. He went on to explain that the river had saved his town, for though the wind had carried the flames across, the townsfolk had fought relentlessly and had succeeded in preventing them from taking hold in that community.

The Haverills listened as he talked on, telling them that, though the town itself was largely spared, Chatham had suffered its own losses. The black clouds of smoke that hung heavy in the air after the fire overcame most of the livestock and a good number of the cattle had suffocated and died.

"We thought we'd all meet with the same fate," Charles added. "We had to dig holes and press our faces to the ground. That gave us a little clean air from the freshly turned earth. Enough to spare us, anyway."

The survivors from Newcastle were not strangers to these details, for they, too, had watched cattle that had survived the fire die later, and they had been forced to take the same measures in order to breathe.

"Some of the ships were saved by the efforts of their crews and nothing less," reported the brother, "but the *Concord*, the *Canada*, and the brig *Jane* were all burnt to the water's edge."

"That they were," his brother said, his voice solemn. "But it's the loss of life that's worst of all."

"Do they have any idea ... how many?" Logan Haverill asked. Beside him, Hannah stiffened as she waited to hear the answer.

"It's too early to say just yet," said the boat's owner. "Some say as many as four hundred, others less than a hundred. It lies somewhere in between, I'd allow."

As the boat moved further and further away, Skye wondered if they would ever be returning to Newcastle. It seemed unlikely, with nothing to go back to. She thought of her home and how safe she had felt there, wrapped in a quilt, snuggled by the warm hearth where winter's cold and wind could not touch her.

There is no house now, she thought. No house or barn or yard; no huge maple tree in the backyard where Tavish and I played as children.

The thought of her brother made Skye's chest hurt. She said yet another prayer for him and Uncle William and Stewart and Abby. Then, fearing she could not keep tears from coming, she pushed those thoughts out of her mind and tried to concentrate on the boat's slow progress toward Chatham.

After what seemed a very long time, they finally reached the docks of their neighbouring town, where Logan hoped to secure temporary lodging for his family. Beyond that, he was at a loss as to what they were going to do.

As they stood on the dock, other survivors from the north side of the river continued to pour into Chatham.

"There are so many of us!" Hannah said, her voice heavy with despair. "Here we are, just a few among such a large number of wounded and hungry stragglers. And all of us needing food and shelter. How can the people of Chatham possibly find room for everyone?"

"Room will be found, of that you can be sure," answered a man nearby. "What kind of neighbours would we be if we failed to offer every possible assistance?"

As willing as they might be to help, Logan couldn't help thinking that the people of Chatham could not possibly feed and house those who had been left impoverished. There could be no fewer than three thousand left homeless from the ravaged communities. The people of the lone surviving town would have laid up winter supplies enough for their own needs only; there was no way they could support so many others, too.

Heads bent with weariness, they began to move away from the dock. Skye thought it miraculous that Chatham's buildings stood, practically unscathed, such a short distance from the destruction on the other side of the river.

And then, just as it seemed something was about to get better, a new wave of terror came. The atmosphere grew ominously dark and cinders began to fall. It seemed as though a second attack was about to come. Panic raced through the crowd.

Skye could see fear and weariness in the faces around her as the people of Chatham prepared themselves to fight the elements once again. There was shouting and bustle in the streets as arrangements were made for men to keep watch and send out a warning if a second storm should materialize.

The Haverills continued through the commotion, following a stooped man whose duty was to take groups arriving from the other side of the river to homes. His slow movements were suited to the task, for they fit the weariness of the refugees as they shuffled toward the promise of food and shelter and hope.

It was cold and the air smelled and tasted bitter. Somewhere nearby, a child began to cry — a loud and anguished wail that seemed inconsolable. Skye swallowed hard several times, wishing that she, too, could give in, could howl and moan and pound something with her fists in anguish and protest.

Instead, she stood quietly beside her father. At his other side, his arm gave support to Hannah and the baby. A girl, Skye thought vaguely, as though this tiny creature was no real part of her world. That the red, wrinkled face belonged to her half-sister had not yet settled in her.

What daylight there was had gone by the time a home had been found for the weary family. At last, the Haverills found themselves in the kitchen of Fay Chapman, a short, somewhat stout woman with a square face and pronounced brow. After putting rough blankets around each of them and adding a log to the fireplace, she clucked and fussed about, serving them porridge and tea along with bannock and molasses.

"I've a clothes chest in the loft with some spare things," she said as she bustled about.

Skye looked down at her dressing gown, now filthy and torn, and thought how wonderful it would be to put on something clean and warm. Even with a blanket around her shoulders and a warm fire nearby, she felt as though she would never stop shivering!

"I'll see what I can find for the baby, first," Mrs. Chapman told Hannah, refilling their mugs with more steaming tea. She could see that the poor creature was naked except for the thin blanket wrapped around her body. "Why, the wee thing can't be more than a few days old!"

Hannah nodded and told her that her new daughter had been born during the long night of the fire.

"You've been through enough, I'll wager," Mrs. Chapman said with a shake of her head. "But you're alive, and that's reason enough for thanks at the moment."

Hannah nodded woodenly, but then her head dropped and it was clear that she was trying very hard to keep from sobbing.

"Have you lost others?" Mrs. Chapman asked kindly, coming to Hannah's side.

"No ... That is, we don't know," Hannah said quietly. "We've two other children. Boys. We do not know if the good Lord has seen fit to spare them."

"They weren't with you when the fire came?" Mrs. Chapman asked.

"No, they were over at the lumberyard, with ...," Hannah began. She could get no further.

"My brother, Collin, was with them," Logan Haverill said, picking up where his wife had left off. "He'd have seen to them, you can be sure of that."

"Well, of course he would!" cried Mrs. Chapman, as though she'd known Collin Haverill her whole life and could vouch for his reliability. She turned to Hannah and patted her hand reassuringly. "They'll be along anytime, you just wait and see."

Skye thought of Tavish and Stewart. They *had* to be all right. It just couldn't be that the last time she had seen them would be the last time she would *ever* see them.

She could not even bear to think of Uncle William, deep in the woods in a lumber camp. What chance would he and the other men there have had when even those near the river had barely escaped with their lives?

CHAPTER EIGHT

They were still getting settled in the Chapman home when Mr. Chapman came in from his chores accompanied by a Mr. Dalton Cullwick. Apparently, Mr. Cullwick had been staying with another family some distance off — a family he lost no time in abusing with one insult after the other. The tick he'd been supplied wouldn't serve for a dog, the food was better fit for pigs — if even pigs would eat it — the people were unpleasant, their children were ill-behaved, and, what was worst of all, judging by the attention it received from Mr. Cullwick, their rum seemed to have been watered down.

"I told the missus, 'Good woman, if I want water, I'll go to the well!'" he'd said, his voice full of indignation.

Mistaking the stunned silence in the room for sympathy, Mr. Cullwick expounded further on the things he'd suffered — in a home that had been kind enough to take him in!

Equally shocking was his treatment of his new hosts. Skye was appalled as he made it abundantly clear that he was accustomed to much finer lodgings than those in which he presently found himself.

"Nevertheless," he added, in a failed attempt at humility, "under the circumstances, I can bear a few inconveniences with good grace — and will do so if you can arrange private sleeping quarters, for I have never been able to rest adequately in a common room."

Skye was not alone in her disgust of this detestable man, but no one raised a voice to chasten him for his bad manners. Rather, Mrs. Chapman told him he was welcome to stay with them until something more suitable could be arranged — an offer she was obliged to make under the circumstances, for the hour was very late and the idea of turning anyone out — even someone as disagreeable as Mr. Cullwick — would never enter her mind.

The next morning saw no improvement in the unpleasant guest. Beginning each sentence with the falsehood that he didn't like to complain, Mr. Cullwick managed to find fault with a number of things, including the bed he'd been provided and the breakfast Mrs. Chapman had prepared.

It had looked as though Mr. Chapman might be about to speak up but instead, lips clamped tight, he had pushed himself away from the table and headed out to begin his day. Logan Haverill rose at once and accompanied him, eager to make himself useful to his host.

Skye was shocked to see that Mr. Cullwick showed no sign of doing the same. Instead, he offered a heavy sigh and commented that he didn't suppose there was any decent reading material in the home.

"We've a Bible," Mrs. Chapman replied meekly.

"An *excellent* choice," Hannah said from the corner, where she sat nursing the baby. Her face was impassive, but Skye could see a spark in her eyes.

"In fact, I was looking for something, ah, more modern," Mr. Cullwick said. Then he turned haughtily toward Hannah. "I do hope, madam, that you didn't mean to suggest that I am in need of spiritual fortification."

"By no means," Hannah said. "The Bible is always a good choice, but in our present state of distress, it is even more fitting. Do you not agree?"

"Yes, of course," Cullwick said, "only at the moment I was hoping to be distracted by something a little more fanciful."

While Cullwick was complaining, most of the town's inhabitants were offering prayers of thanks, for, in spite of the threat of another storm the evening before, no further calamity had come and, in fact, the smoke had begun to abate.

It was through this clearing air that Skye Haverill, looking rather odd, made her way toward the docks in Chatham.

She had been glad to exchange her filthy nightdress for warm, decent daywear, but the heavy woollen dress that had been provided for her had clearly belonged to Mrs. Chapman herself and was ill-fitting, to say the least. It was both too short and too loose on the young girl's slender form, which made it resemble a brown sack whose contents had been half emptied. Even tying it at the waist with a braided length of yarn had done little to improve its appearance.

A grey scarf on her head and a shawl about her shoulders added protection from the elements, but their style was matronly and more fitting for a grandmother than a girl of fourteen.

Even less flattering were the shoes that now adorned her feet. It had turned out that the only footwear that could be spared for her was an old pair of boots once worn by Mr. Chapman. They did nothing to enhance the outfit, and although the extra pair of thick, woollen socks that kept them from falling right off her feet actually made them cozy and warm, Skye found little comfort in this benefit.

She could have stayed inside and spared herself from public scrutiny, but two things made her willing to endure the embarrassment.

First and foremost was her desire to know what had become of Tavish and Stewart. It was only because her father and stepmother shared this longing that she had been permitted to venture out at all. Although they'd allowed her to go, both had cautioned her to restrict her walk to the dock and back, and to watch carefully for any sign of trouble.

Her second reason for going was to escape from the insufferable Mr. Cullwick!

She had nearly reached her destination when a voice reached her.

"Skye!"

Turning to the sound of her name, Skye saw a familiar figure coming toward her. "Emily!" she cried, throwing open her arms and stepping forward to meet her friend. "I'm so glad to see you."

"And I you," Emily said as they hugged.

"Your family? Are they all safe?" Skye asked.

"Yes. And yours?"

"Tavish and Stewart were with Uncle Collin when the fire came. Uncle William was working in a lumber camp, so it will be a few days at least before there's news of him," Skye said.

"You've heard nothing at all?"

"No, but I'm even now on my way to the docks to wait for them, or word of them."

"I'll come along with you," Emily said. Her voice fell to a whisper and she spoke again. "Did you hear about Mary?"

"Mary Taylor? No. What news do you have of her?"

"Mary and the two youngest." Emily's eyes filled with tears and her voice broke. She drew a breath and managed to add, "All three perished."

"No!" Shock immobilized Skye. "Are you certain?"

"I heard it from her sister-in-law, Ellen. Mary was carrying the little ones, Edward and Elijah, running toward the marshes, when she stumbled and fell. It seemed she twisted her ankle in the fall, and was unable to continue with enough speed to outrun the fire. Ellen saw the whole thing, but she had her own baby to carry and couldn't stop to help."

Mary and her two little brothers, dead ... burned alive! It was too much to bear. Tears spilled freely as Skye and Emily wept in each other's arms.

When they could speak again, the pair vowed that they would never forget their friend.

CHAPTER NINE

Skye and Emily were surprised to see a small crowd of people already gathered at the docks in Chatham.

"These aren't dock workers," Skye observed.

It would be quite normal to see men waiting to load or unload a ship, but there was no ship in sight, and in any case, the group before them was clearly not there for this purpose. A mix of young and old men and women as well as children of all ages had assembled there.

"Something must be going on," Emily said, stepping a little closer to her friend without even realizing it.

"So it would seem," Skye agreed, "and yet, I see no activity of any sort to explain their presence."

"We'll know soon enough," Emily said, and she was right, for they were quickly nearing the little gathering.

Skye was glad her friend was with her. She would never have made inquiries on her own, but Emily, as soon as they had reached the crowd, hastened to ask its purpose of a woman who stood holding an infant and clutching a toddler's hand.

"Why are we here?" the woman said, echoing Emily's question as though she could barely take in its meaning. "Why, we're here in the hope of news of family and friends, child. Why are *you* here?"

The girls were a trifle embarrassed that they hadn't realized it immediately. Naturally, if they had come in search of some report on Tavish and Stewart, others would be there for a like purpose.

This was even more evident as they looked closer, saw a few familiar faces, and realized that some of the group was made up of persons from Newcastle. Many were as oddly dressed as Skye, with garments clearly intended for others.

Observing the lot it was not difficult to guess that they had something in common, for their expressions were strikingly similar. For the most part, hope and apprehension blended on their faces, although one emotion or the other would prevail now and then.

Skye and Emily drifted off to the side of the group, and each girl shared her story of the past few days. There were similarities, of course, but differences, too.

Skye listened with rapt attention as Emily described how her family had raced to the river and begun swimming for the far shore.

"We'd never have made it — not one of us," she declared, "for the water was so rough from the storm, and the distance too great for any of us to manage.

"Father was supporting Jacob on his back, and Mother was doing her best to help little Louise and keep an eye on the rest of us, but then Jacob began to panic and it was all chaos after that.

"By then we saw that we couldn't make the south bank, so once Father got Jacob calmed we swam toward a ship that was out on the water and less than a quarter of a mile from where we then found ourselves.

"Twice more Jacob began to flail, and twice more we had to stop. Mother was holding Louise with one arm by this time and swimming on one side, and we were every one of us just barely managing to keep on. Thank goodness Father always insisted that we all learned to swim well!"

"I'm such a poor swimmer — I'd never have made it any distance," Skye said. As she spoke, her brother's face came to her and she pushed away the thought that he could barely swim a stroke. She forced her attention back to Emily's story.

"Well! We reached the ship at last, but when we did I thought for sure we would perish there, for the crew was busy to a man, fighting desperately to keep it from catching fire. Balls of flame hurled through the air and it seemed they would surely lose their battle to save their vessel. It was a moment such as I never hope to see again, with Newcastle aflame behind us, the far shore beyond our reach, and our only hope looking as though it too would be devoured by the fire and storm.

"How did you come to safety?" Skye asked, her heart beating hard — as though her friend was, even now, in the great peril of which she spoke.

"The crew! Oh, good men, and brave!" cried Emily. "Seeing us there, several of their members exerted themselves to rescue us from the water. They did so at the peril of their ship and even their very lives."

Emily paused, tears filling her eyes, and then she described the determination on the face of the weathered seaman who had gotten her to the safety of the deck. It had been, she said, the look of a man who would not see another perish even if it meant his own life must be lost in the effort. He had not even lingered long enough to hear Emily's hoarse "thank you" before hastening back to the fight to save the vessel and, in the confusion and bustle, she had not seen him again between that time and the moment they found themselves delivered to the docks in Chatham, where she stood once more.

"You haven't seen Newcastle then," Skye said.

"No, but we've heard there is little left of it, and that the dead are strewn from one end to the other."

"They are," Skye confirmed sadly. "And I fear that one of those is a girl who had been staying with us. Do you remember Abby Gunn? She worked for the Carpenters but they had loaned her to us for the harvest."

"Abby? Yes, I remember her. But why do you think her lost? She is even now at a house not far from where my family is staying."

"Are you *sure?*" Skye's heart quickened with joy at the thought.

Emily nodded. "I saw her yesterday, digging in the ground like the rest of us to catch a clean breath of air. Thank goodness the smoke is clearing today."

A boat was arriving and the girls fell silent and watched as a small, bedraggled group disembarked and came slowly across the dock.

There were a few cries of joy as those waiting saw loved ones, feared dead, coming toward them. They clasped each other and cried out their thanks and went off, arm-in-arm.

For others, news was shared that confirmed the worst, and then there were moans and wrenching sobs. With no further reason to stand watch, mourners departed, some supported by kind arms, others walking alone.

Skye thought she had never seen a more lonely sight than that of an older woman who had just been given news that her husband was dead. The way she shuffled along with her head bowed and her shoulders stooped, it seemed as though she was shrinking into herself a little more with each step. Now and then she stopped and dabbed at her tired, old eyes.

"So, what about your family?"

Skye's attention was drawn back by Emily's question and she realized she hadn't yet told of her own family's escape from the fire.

Emily was surprised to hear Skye speak of Hannah without the usual ill will, and when Skye told her how her stepmother had saved her life, Emily clasped her hands tightly and became so filled with emotion that she could not speak.

Then Skye got to the part about Hannah giving birth on the raft while the heavens roared above her and the water raged below.

"You have a sister!" Emily squealed, hugging her friend.

"A *sister*," Skye echoed while the word sank in. It *is* my sister, she thought in wonder. A smile crept onto her face.

A sister! In the past she had envied some of her friends who had sisters even though she'd heard mixed reports on this particular blessing. The idea that the tiny creature who had arrived in the midst of such turmoil was indeed her sister hadn't quite struck her before — no doubt because, in her mind, she had kept Hannah separate from the rest of the family.

The morning passed slowly, even though the two friends had much to tell each other. More and more boats came and unloaded their weary cargo. Some travelled alone, others in small groups.

The scene from the first boat was played out again and again. As the day went by, the group that gathered at the docks changed continuously as people came and left from both sides of the river.

The homes in Chatham, though they were already bulging, turned no one away.

By mid afternoon, the girls were hungry, but Skye was unwilling to leave. After trying for some time to persuade her, Emily gave up and decided that enduring a little hunger was better than leaving her friend to watch and wait alone.

And then, just as daylight began to fade, a familiar face appeared. Skye's heart gave a happy skip when she saw that it was one of the boys.

"At last," she cried. "It's them!" Skye gave Emily a quick hug before turning back to greet the pair.

But then, even as her hand rose in a wave, something inside her felt suddenly cold and scared.

Only *one* boy was making his way out of the boat and crossing the dock to where she stood.

CHAPTER TEN

Skye tried to smile as she stepped forward to greet Stewart, but her face wouldn't obey. Barely able to breathe, she struggled to overcome the fear that gripped her as if mighty hands were squeezing her chest.

"Skye, you're safe!" Stewart cried, clasping her to him for a brief moment. He drew back then and cleared his throat. "Our parents ... Are they ...?"

"They're fine, both of them," Skye answered quickly. Never once had it crossed her mind that the boys would have been wondering about *them*, and yet it was only natural that they would.

"And Tavish?" she managed, though it was difficult to force the question out, so constricted was her throat from fear.

"Tavish didn't come across," Stewart said slowly. His eyes dropped away from looking at her, and Skye knew instantly that something was dreadfully wrong.

"You must tell me at once!" she cried. "Is he alive?"

"Alive? Oh, yes!" Stewart reached out and took hold of Skye's arm, steadying her as she sagged with relief.

"And he's well?"

Stewart hesitated, then said, reluctantly, "It seems the fire affected his eyes." He took a deep breath. "He can't see."

"Can't see!" Skye gasped. "You mean, he's blind?"

"We won't know for certain until a doctor can be found for him, but he's not been able to see since the night of the fire."

Skye could hardly sort out her feelings quickly enough. Of course, the most important thing was that Tavish was alive, but the thought of her brother without his sight ... Skye shook her head and pushed it aside, unprepared to think about it just then. At last, she said, "Except for that, is he all right?"

"As much as any of us," Stewart said.

"Why did he not come across with you?"

"He wouldn't leave Collin."

"Uncle Collin!" Skye found herself blushing with embarrassment. She hadn't even thought to inquire after her uncle and his family. "Are he and his family all right?"

Stewart didn't answer at once, and in that brief silence Skye knew that whatever he was about to say would be grave news. Her hand automatically reached for her friend and Emily grasped it tightly.

"Collin alone was spared."

"No!"

"I'm dreadfully sorry, Skye. I wish I had better news."

Skye hardly heard his words. Images of Aunt Susan and the boys — her cousins Adam, Kenneth, and Duncan — rushed and tumbled through her mind's eye. Duncan, the baby of the family, had just begun to walk when she'd last seen him, and Skye had taken particular delight in watching him toddle from person to person, clearly excited about his newfound ability.

"There's no chance that this is a mistake?" she managed after a moment.

"I'm afraid not. They never got out of the house," Stewart said quietly. "Collin, Tavish, and I couldn't get to them before the fire came. We tried, but the flames were on the house before we could reach it. We barely reached the river in time ourselves."

"But how do you know *absolutely*?" Skye cried. "Is it not *possible* that they made their way to safety without your knowledge?"

Stewart drew a deep breath and then, with some reluctance, told her, "They were found, Skye. I'm afraid there's no question that they perished."

Skye broke down, collapsing against Emily. Her friend's arms encircled her as she sobbed broken-heartedly.

"There now," Emily said softly. Tears filled her own eyes as she witnessed Skye's grief.

Stewart reached a hand out and awkwardly patted his stepsister's arm. He was thankful that she had not been there with them when the bodies were found, for the sight was a horror he felt he would see every day for the rest of his life, and one that he wouldn't have wanted Skye to have to endure.

Sleeping or not when the fire came, Susan and the children had most certainly been awake when it swallowed their home and snuffed out their lives. They had been found huddled together, arms clasped about each other in what must have been a final, desperate bid for comfort or relief. Even so, no one who had seen the charred remains of this death embrace could be in any doubt that they had died most horribly, for their final contortions had most certainly been caused by great agony.

"Uncle Collin," Skye said when she could speak again. "How is he?"

"He's about as you'd expect, I suppose," Stewart said. "He's spoken but little since it happened."

"And is there ..." Skye hesitated, swallowing hard. She felt she could not bear any more bad news, but could not keep herself from asking, "Is there any news yet of the men in the camps? Of Uncle William?"

"Not of William. I've heard that one or two men have come in from the woods," Stewart told her, "but their camps were not so far off. Still, there's reason to hope. He could appear at any time."

Uncle William *must* be all right, Skye told herself as she had done many times since the night of the fire. Even so, her heart sank to hear that there was no news and she had to remind herself firmly that it was simply too early. Only those working nearby would have had any chance to return to Newcastle so quickly.

"We must go to Father," Skye said. It seemed to her that Logan Haverill would somehow help make things right, although there was no logic behind this idea. She knew only that her father had always been strong and able and she turned to him instinctively during times of trouble.

The three began walking back toward the Chapmans'. Emily remained with Skye and Stewart until they reached the house, but did not go in.

"I just wanted to know where I could find you again," she told Skye before turning back the way they'd just come.

Skye and Stewart had almost reached the door when she realized that he didn't yet know about the baby.

"I almost forgot to tell you, your mother's time came the night of the fire," she said. "She had a baby girl."

"And Mother? Is she okay?"

"Yes. Tired, as you'd expect, but otherwise she seems fine."

"The baby is all right, too?"

"Yes."

"Another sister," Stewart said. A smile flashed. "A

smaller one this time."

His words surprised Skye and, oddly, brought tears to her eyes. In the year since their parents had married she had become fond of Stewart, but she had stubbornly refused to think of him as a brother. That he looked at her as his sister in spite of that had not occurred to her before.

There was no time to think of that, though, for looking up she saw her father, who had spied Stewart and was now striding toward them from the direction of the barn.

Seconds later, Hannah came running from the house, her face lit up with joy at the sight of her son. She threw her arms around him and kissed him, but then she stepped back, looking about. The colour drained from her face.

"Where is *Tavish*?" she cried. "*Stewart*! *Where* is Tavish?"

Skye watched as Stewart repeated what he had told her just a short time earlier. It struck her that a stranger observing the scene would never have guessed that Hannah was not really Tavish's mother.

CHAPTER ELEVEN

Even though her father rarely showed emotion, Skye could see that the news hit him very hard. After hearing Stewart's account of how the fire had taken the lives of his sister-in-law and three nephews, Logan slipped away from the others.

Skye saw him seated on a small log pile not far from the house. She was about to join him, but she stepped back into the shadows when she saw Hannah approaching from the house.

"I've brought you a cup of tea," Hannah said softly as she passed her husband the steaming cup.

"Thanks."

"I'm deeply sorry for your losses, Logan," she added in the same quiet voice. "And for the news of Tavish, though I'm thankful that he's safe at least."

Logan nodded but said nothing. Moments passed with no further exchange and then Skye saw Hannah's hand rise from her side and reach toward Logan. It moved slowly, hesitantly, as though she wanted to touch him but didn't quite have the courage. When her fingers finally reached him, they lighted on his shoulder for no more than a second or two and then drew away.

When Hannah returned to the house, Skye went to join her father. She sat next to him and for a few moments there was silence.

"I don't know where to turn, Skye," he said suddenly. "I've always counted myself a believer, but sometimes the words just don't want to come when I try to pray."

"Mrs. Webber —." Skye's voice caught as soon as the name left her lips. She felts tears forming again at the thought of the pastor's wife, and had to clear her throat before she could continue. "Mrs. Webber once said that she thought some of the best prayers she ever prayed had no words to them at all. She said they were the ones that went up right out of her heart, before her head could spoil them with words."

"There's wisdom in that," Logan said, nodding. "Collin and Tavish will be needing to hear words such as those."

"When will we be able to see them?"

"I mean to go there before the week is out," Logan answered. "One thing is sure: there's plenty of room on the boats going that way."

"Can I come?" Even as she asked, Skye knew the answer.

"You can't, Skye. You've seen what's over there. It's no longer a fit place for man nor beast."

Skye wanted to plead, but she knew her father wouldn't bend. His thoughts were shifting anyway, as he noticed Skye trembling.

"Come now. You're cold, child," he said, standing. "Best if we go in."

Mrs. Chapman came hurrying over the minute they'd stepped inside. "We've heard the dreadful news," she cried. "Nathan and I are so sorry for your loss."

"Thank you."

"Your poor, poor brother!" she continued. "To have lost his whole family. You can be sure we'll pray for him. And for your boy!"

"My sympathies to you as well, Mr. Haverill." Dalton Cullwick said. Mr. Cullwick was sitting in a chair digesting the liberal portion of dinner he'd eaten — though he'd spent the entire meal offering Mrs. Chapman suggestions on how she might improve the dish when she next made it.

"Yes, thank you."

"Come, sit by the fire," Mrs. Chapman said. "Perhaps we can read a Psalm together."

Logan started to do as he was bidden but, as he passed Hannah, he paused to look down at his new daughter, swaddled and asleep in her arms. It occurred to him that the child, as yet, had no name.

"Have you thought of what you'd like to call her?"

he asked his wife.

"I'd been thinking of 'Elizabet,'" Hannah answered, "after Reverend Webber's wife, rest her soul. She was a good person, and kind. But now, I don't know."

"It's a good choice," he said.

"But perhaps ... well, I was wondering if you'd prefer 'Susan.'"

"It would mean something to Collin," Logan allowed. "But either one would be all right."

"Why not ...," Skye's voice trailed off. She looked down, embarrassed at having started to blurt her opinion when it clearly wasn't her place to interfere.

"What is it, Skye?" Hannah asked.

"I was just thinking ... it was only a passing idea ...," Skye said. "I thought maybe you could use both."

"Both? 'Susan Elizabet'? Or 'Elizabet Susan'?"

"'Elizabet Susan,'" Logan spoke up unexpectedly. "It sounds fine."

And so it was that Skye's new sister was named, on her suggestion, for two women who had lost their lives on the same night that the young child's began.

CHAPTER TWELVE

On the north side of the river, Tavish Haverill lay awake. All around him were the sounds of people snoring, many of them in restless slumber.

The home he was in was one of the few that had been spared — a crudely built house in a low, almost swampy area. The flames had raced over and past it as they rushed along their path of destruction.

The couple that owned the dwelling were Matilda and Hiram Savoy. They'd done their best for the group that had made its way to the unlikely sanctuary, but their provisions were fast disappearing.

Tavish knew none of this, nor had he seen the room he shared, at that moment, with his uncle and nine others. From the morning after the fire, when he and Stewart and Uncle Collin had dragged themselves from the river, he had realized that something was wrong.

"The air's as thick and black as night," he'd said.

Even as he spoke, he felt something cold inside him, something that told him there was more to it.

"It's the ash," Stewart answered. "It's hard to see, all right."

"Hard!" Tavish said. "Why, it's like walking in the thickest, darkest fog ever."

Something in his tone made Stewart turn to face him, and the younger boy was shocked to realize that the way Tavish was staring sightlessly could only mean one thing.

He drew Uncle Collin aside and told him what he suspected, and in short order it was clear to all three that Tavish was indeed blind.

And he wasn't the only one. Before long, they'd encountered three others who'd lost their sight. Like the others, Tavish was forced to take hold of an arm — mainly Stewart's — and be led along like a child. But then, a few days earlier Stewart had gone over to Chatham and Uncle Collin had no time to guide him about.

Then, that afternoon, when they'd been outside, Tavish had heard the jubilant cry of an old woman. It was what she said that drew his attention.

"I can see! I can see!"

Tavish had edged toward her, feeling his way along while Uncle Collin was off with several other men, checking some trees that remained standing.

"Did I hear you say that you can see?"

"It's a miracle!" the high, thin voice cried. "I've

been blind for days, but now I can see!"

Tavish had carried her words, had heard them over and over in the hours that had passed since he'd spoken to the old woman.

He wanted to pray — to beg God for this same miracle: the restoration of his sight — but he hadn't been able to let the words form in his mouth.

How can I think of myself when so many are suffering and dead around me? he thought. How can I think of myself when I don't know whether my father and Skye and Hannah ... and Abby ... are even alive.

And his questions drifted to the uncertainty of the future, and what it could possibly hold for them, cast as they were, as beggars on the world.

The questions that plagued Tavish Haverill as he grappled for sleep that night were far from uncommon in the settlements of Miramichi, New Brunswick. The same uncertainty echoed in the minds of some twenty-five hundred settlers left destitute by the fire.

What will become of us?

How will we survive?

Without homes, food, or even clothing to keep and sustain them during the rapidly approaching winter, the situation seemed hopeless indeed. They knew that they could not possibly live off their neighbouring town for any length of time without depleting its resources to a dangerous level.

Nor could the crowded living arrangements last for long. Even those possessing the most pleasant of dispositions would find it difficult to bear the intrusion for the long, dark months of winter. It could not be many weeks before tempers were frayed and the good will, so freely and willingly extended, turned to discord and resentment.

And how could it be otherwise? Is it possible to sustain any degree of charity while strangers consume the food meant to ensure the survival of one's children, and in so doing jeopardize the survival of all?

There were many murmured conversations and anxious prayers that night, but the situation seemed hopeless. It was readily apparent to both sufferers and supporters that if a long-term solution was to be had, it was not going to be found in the town of Chatham.

At the Chapman home, both homeowners and guests were treated to Mr. Cullwick's thoughts on the matter — opinions which, in Skye's estimation, they could all have done quite nicely without.

"Such difficulties as may lie ahead," he intoned, "must simply be borne with courage and the willingness for hard work. After all, adversity builds character."

"And what about yourself, Mr. Cullwick?" Hannah asked, her face a mask of politeness. "What deprivations do *you* expect to endure in order that *your* character might be likewise enriched?"

"Well, of course you can appreciate the difference

of my circumstances," he answered immediately, with his usual, self-important air. "After all, I was born a gentleman, and am entitled to the considerations of my position."

"How fortunate for you to be deserving of such privilege — and all by virtue of your birth," Hannah said.

Mr. Cullwick's eyes narrowed. Even someone as self-absorbed as he was couldn't entirely miss the undertone of contempt in Hannah's words, although she spoke in a civil manner.

"Yes, well," was all he said by way of reply before his voice trailed off and he turned his face toward the fire.

Skye wondered how anyone could have so little compassion for others, and once again felt the urge to get away from the disagreeable man. She asked Hannah if she and Stewart could go for a walk through town. Permission was given much more readily than it had been the previous day, although it came with similar warnings to be watchful.

"What is it we're to be watchful for?" Stewart asked as the two started along the road. "It's not as though there's going to be another fire."

"How can you be so sure?"

"For one thing, everything's already burned as far as you can see along the north side of the river."

"But not on this side," Skye said. Even uttering the words made her feel uneasy and she glanced around as though the nightmare she'd lived through only days before might be about to repeat itself.

"Aw, such a thing we've just seen wouldn't happen twice in ten lifetimes," Stewart said.

"I suppose not," Skye agreed, "but then, until a few days ago I'd never have thought such a thing was possible at all."

Stewart glanced sideways at her. "Do you think it was a judgement, like some people say?"

"I don't know. Maybe."

"Tavish told me he heard an old man going about crying out that it was a warning from God."

"A warning?" Skye echoed.

"Yes — a glimpse of what hell would be like for us all if we didn't repent and turn from our wicked ways."

"Do you think our ways are wicked, Stewart?" Skye asked.

"I don't suppose the people here are any worse than people anywhere else," he said after a moment's thought.

Skye had nothing to add to that and the two walked along in silence for a few moments. After a bit, they reached the house where Emily was staying and, as if they'd already agreed on it, turned on the path toward the door.

But it was Mrs. Russell who came to the door, with the news that Emily had taken ill.

"It's the fever," she told them, "and it's impossible to get a doctor. They can't begin to keep up with those that need them as it is, with so many sick and injured from the fire."

"She'll be all right, don't you worry" Stewart told Skye as they made their way along the street afterward. "Emily's young and healthy. Them that die from the fever are mostly really young or very old."

Before Skye could answer him, a man came into sight calling out that a meeting was now underway at the home of a Chatham resident. The shouted announcement made it clear that the meeting's purpose was to find ways in which they might deal with the disaster that had left the area in a state of emergency.

"Where is this place?" Stewart asked the man as they met.

"You'll see it well enough by the number of gigs standing by," came the reply. "Just keep on this way. But you'll not gain admission, lad. I'm afraid it's a business matter — men only."

Stewart looked so crestfallen that the man added, "Still, if you wait nearby you'll hear enough to satisfy you, I'll wager."

"You'd best go back to the house," Stewart told Skye after thanking the man. "I'm on to see what I can find out about this meeting."

Skye did as he suggested, though she was just as curious as he was to find out what was taking place. As she retraced her steps, several small children burst into view, running and giggling. And few steps behind them, looking far less pleased with the game, was Abby.

"Skye?" she cried out, seeing the younger girl. "Thank the good Lord you're alive. I thought you'd perished that dreadful night!"

"And I feared the worst for you," Skye admitted, hugging Abby as they reached each other. "But Emily Russell gave me news of you yesterday."

"Your family?" Abby asked. "Are they ...?"

"Yes, all."

"Hannah and your father are safe, then? And the boys?" Abby said, colouring a little as she repeated her inquiries. "You all made it to Chatham?"

"Father and Hannah and Stewart and I are all here, staying at a home but a short ways off," Skye said. "Tavish is still in Newcastle." She went on to tell Abby about the tragedy to her Uncle Collin's family, and finished with the news that Tavish had lost his sight the night of the fire.

Abby shook her head sadly as she listened. "There's been so much loss and tragedy," she said at last, "I don't know how the town can ever recover."

"Do you think Newcastle will ever be built again?" Skye asked, pulling her thoughts away from the fate her aunt and cousins had suffered.

"I don't see how. There's almost nothing left."

Skye had to agree that the situation looked quite hopeless. It seemed that her beloved town was gone forever.

CHAPTER THIRTEEN

Tavish blinked slowly and wondered if he was imagining things. Several times that day it had seemed that there was a perceptible difference in the dark haze that had swallowed his sight. Was it really lighter than it had been the day before, or was he just trying to convince himself of it?

A sudden surge of fear ran through him but Tavish couldn't quite identify *why* he was afraid. It was a few moments before it hit him. The thing that he feared was hope. He thought back to the moment when he'd realized that his eyes were no longer working. It had felt as though he'd been struck by a blow.

Blind! The shock of it was a palpable jolt inside him and his heart had beat it out over and over, pumping the word through his body like some horrible refrain.

"Blind ... blind ... blind ... blind ... blind."

He felt sure he couldn't face the agony of those

moments again, even though the initial distress had settled, after a bit, into a sickening, hollow feeling of self-pity. It had been several days before he'd managed to fight it — his battle brought on by shame as he heard the cries of those around him, many of whom had suffered far greater losses than that of sight.

His Uncle Collin, whom Tavish refused to leave even though he longed to seek news of his own family, was a strange support for the young man. Tavish couldn't see his uncle, yet he felt the strength and courage in countless ways as Collin pushed forward in spite of the horrible loss he had suffered.

The first example had been the manner in which Collin had laid his family to rest. Tavish had been unable to help as the graves were dug in the corner of what had once been the field where Susan and the boys had gardened together. He sat nearby, his frustration growing with the sound of each strike of the shovel Uncle Collin had fashioned for this purpose.

It had been the relentless thrust of that shovel through the soot and into the earth that had begun to erase the self-pity building in Tavish. Every shovelfull of soil fell like a reprimand and before the day was out, Tavish's own loss had begun to seem much less significant to him.

As much as was possible in the space of a few days, Tavish had resigned himself to his condition and had resolved to accept it like a man. Except, now it seemed as though there was some small improvement, and the thought that perhaps his sight would return caused hope to stir in his breast.

And it was this very hope that frightened him. He knew that if he dared to hope, he risked facing disappointment and might have to deal with his condition all over again.

But *was* that an outline of something? Were the shadows a lighter grey? Or was his mind playing tricks on him?

Tavish closed his eyes and blocked out the little light that had filtered through.

Across the river at that evening's meal, Elizabet Susan Haverill was being much admired by all at the Chapman table. (The tiny cause of celebration was herself asleep and quite oblivious to her role in bringing pleasure to the group.)

It seemed that the infant's crying had begun to disturb Mr. Dalton Cullwick, and in fact, had caused him such undue stress that he had determined to find more suitable lodgings.

"Mrs. Chapman, I do hope you will not take offence at what I am about to say," he had announced earlier. "In spite of your commendable efforts, I fear I must take my leave of your home."

Cullwick leaned forward and lowered his voice, though it still carried to where Hannah sat with her baby.

"The sad truth is, that squalling infant prevents me from all enjoyment when I'm reading, and I am quite unable to achieve any focus in my daily time of contemplation."

Mr. Cullwick's "daily time of contemplation" was, in truth, nothing more than an afternoon nap, something he denied no matter how loudly he might have snored.

"I'm sorry that you feel you've been inconvenienced, Mr. Cullwick," Mrs. Chapman said. "But it *is* only natural for little ones to fuss."

Mr. Cullwick smiled benevolently. "The fault is not yours, madam, I assure you." As he spoke, he darted an accusing look at Hannah, as though to suggest that she had wilfully borne the child for the sole purpose of disturbing him.

"Why, Mr. Cullwick, there is no one to fault over a crying infant."

"Yes, well, in any case, let me assure you that your hospitality has been most satisfactory. Indeed, you'll be pleased to know I've found the shortcomings in your home are hardly worth noting."

And at that, he bowed to his freshly insulted hostess, said his goodbyes, and made off.

"A body almost feels guilty letting him go," Mrs. Chapman said, though her tone was surprisingly cheerful for someone struggling with that emotion.

"How so?" Hannah asked, barely trusting herself to speak. Skye had watched her while Mr. Cullwick complained about the baby, and had marvelled at her stepmother's self-control. Hannah's face had remained impassive the whole time. In fact, the only visible sign of anger had been a heightening of the colour in her cheeks.

"Well," Mrs. Chapman explained, "after all, it's hardly fair to whoever gets him next. I feel as though I ought to warn them."

"But you can't," Hannah said with a smile. "For one thing, you don't know where he's going. And for another, you can't offer a warning without speaking ill of the man."

"I suppose that's true," Mrs. Chapman said cheerfully. Then she crossed the room to where Elizabet Susan lay in her mother's arms, leaned down, and kissed the child.

When the men came in to eat and learned of Mr. Cullwick's departure, they too seemed to experience a surge of affection for the baby. Mr. Chapman commented that she was the loveliest baby he'd ever seen while Logan (who was still somewhat timid about holding his tiny new daughter) carried her about in his arms until she fell asleep.

Skye was certain that Mr. Cullwick could never even have dreamt that his departure from the Chapman home would bring about such a reaction. She decided that anyone who could insult others without even realizing it was also capable of deceiving himself on other matters. No doubt he imagined them sorry to see him go.

CHAPTER FOURTEEN

Everyone looked up as Stewart burst through the door of the Chapman home, his face flushed with excitement.

"Wait until you hear!" he said. "I've just come ..."

"Stewart!" Hannah interrupted. "Where are your manners?"

Stewart stopped long enough to reach his hand up and yank the cap from his head, but the look on his face was more impatient than contrite. He opened his mouth to speak, but was cut off again before he'd even uttered a single word.

"Son," Hannah said firmly, "you don't rush into a house — least of all one where you're a guest — and interrupt whatever conversation may have been going on."

"Now, now," said Mr. Chapman, "we weren't saying anything important in any case."

"And it isn't at all like the boy," Logan added. "Stewart is a fine, polite lad. I'd say whatever news he has must be big."

Stewart's eyes widened a little at that. He glanced at Logan, surprised that his stepfather had defended him. Not that Logan had ever been unkind — but their relationship had been courteous in a distant kind of way, and he hadn't known what manner of opinion his mother's new husband had formed about him.

It made no difference, however, for when Stewart looked at his mother he found the expression on her face unchanged. "Having something to tell is no reason for you to forget to behave as a gentleman," she said.

"Yes'm," Stewart said. His face had reddened a little as he addressed the group. "Excuse me for interrupting."

"Not at all," Mrs. Chapman said, going to the boy and taking his arm. "Come on now and have a seat and tell us what you've heard."

"Well, I went to the house where the meeting was being held and there was already a crowd gathered outside. I thought they might send me off, but no one paid much mind to me until one man came along and asked me some questions. I told him I was from Newcastle and that we'd lost everything in the fire. Then he said if I'd tend to the horses he'd bring me news of what went on inside after the meeting was over.

"It seemed to go on forever, but at last he came out

and made good on his promise, and I've come now with the whole account of it … such as I can recall. There was much to remember.

"It seems that the first order of business was that of taking subscriptions,"* Stewart continued. "More than £800 was raised this very day!"

"What? From the people of Chatham alone?" Logan asked.

"Yes," Stewart said, "but that's not all. The merchants who have large sums outstanding to them from advances made to lumbermen and businessmen have forgiven the debts."

"Forgiven them?" Logan repeated. "But there would be so many debtors — the sums must be immense! Are you certain?" His own obligations had weighed upon him — along with other worries for the future. In his entire life he had never failed to repay a debt in full and on time, regardless of what other hardships he had to face. The thought that he could not possibly do so this time had added to his burden.

"I heard it from the gentleman as sure as I stand before you," Stewart assured him. "He told of how one of the principal men of Chatham stood in the meeting after the subscriptions had been raised. The man thanked God for His bounty and for the mercy He has shown to this town, and said that all those who carried debts

---

* Donations.

to him owed him no more. And then, one by one, the other merchants stood and said the same and declared themselves glad to do so."

Skye felt her eyes misting at the thought of such generosity and kindness — and she was not alone. Logan's throat had gone tight and a sudden ache had sprung into his chest. He clenched his teeth together and set his jaw, determined not to look foolish.

"But that's only the start of it!" Stewart said, "The ships that are in dock are to be detained so that no provisions can leave."

"Has this group power to decree such a thing?" Mr. Chapman asked.

"I believe the gentleman told me that they would recommend this to the magistrates," Stewart explained quickly, anxious to get on with his story.

"Communications are to be sent at once to Fredericton, Saint John, Halifax, Pictou, Prince Edward Island, Quebec, and so on, to spread word of the conflagration and its devastation, and to seek help from all who can provide it."

So many places, thought Skye. But would complete strangers really be willing to help?

"A committee is drawing up the communication to go to His Excellency, Sir Howard Douglas."*

* The Lieutenant-Governor of New Brunswick from March 1823–February 1831, for whom the former Douglastown (now part of the city of Miramichi) was named.

Stewart announced this so proudly that you'd have thought they were acting on his suggestion. The mention of the Lieutenant-Governor brought immediate murmurs of approval from the Chapmans as well as Logan and Hannah. Since his appointment, Sir Douglas's benevolence and dedication had gained him the admiration and trust of the colony.

"But why would they need a committee just to write a letter?" Skye asked.

Stewart searched through his memory of the conversation he'd had a short time earlier. "I think it was so that nothing would be forgotten — as to what things are most needed," he said after a brief pause. "Like, medical help for those with burns and injuries and other illnesses, and provisions and such."

"Sure and they'd need to let His Excellency know how desperate the situation is, how total the destruction, and how great is the suffering at hand," Chapman said with a nod.

"Was there anything else decided at this meeting?" Skye asked, still mildly resentful that she'd been sent home while Stewart went to hear all about it.

"A few things," Stewart said. "They're to make arrangements for the dead to be buried. And they determined that any cattle left without feed are to be purchased at once on the best possible terms, slain, salted, and added to the stock of provisions."

"A wise move," Logan commented.

"That's it," Stewart said. "At least, that's all I can remember."

"They've done so much," Hannah said. "More than most would have thought of or accomplished in a single meeting. We must all pray that those sent to take news of our plight will have a safe journey."

Fay Chapman looked as though she was about to add something to this, but a knock came at the door just then, drawing her attention.

She was still rising to her feet to see who was there when the door swung open. There in the opening (and, if the scowl he wore was any indication, in especially bad humour) was none other than Mr. Dalton Cullwick!

CHAPTER FIFTEEN

"Mr. Cullwick!" Mrs. Chapman sputtered. "But I thought ..."

Cullwick stepped inside and sat down at a bench beside the table. He looked so weary and discouraged that Skye almost felt sorry for him.

"It seems that any accommodations as would be fitting for a gentleman such as myself are completely occupied," he said. "Therefore, I have been compelled to return to your home. But I've made up my mind! I won't have you worrying over the discomforts I may suffer here, for I am determined to bear them with equanimity."

"Perhaps another day," Mrs. Chapman said, trying to hide a sigh.

"Another day?" Cullwick repeated.

"I only meant that you might have better luck

another day. In finding a situation more suited to your station."

"Yes, perhaps," he agreed. But the truth was, Cullwick could not face the thought of another day like the one he had just been through. What misery, trudging from home to home only to be told that there was no place for him. The experience had left him feeling rather insulted and more than a little sorry for himself.

As if *she* was expressing the general feeling over Cullwick's return, Elizabet Susan chose that moment to wake and make it well known to one and all that she was quite ready for her next meal.

Collin Haverill lay awake on the floor near to his nephew, Tavish. He longed for sleep to come, to give him a few hours away from the pain that filled his every waking moment, but even that door of escape seemed closed to him that night.

The days were easier, in spite of everything, for they had become filled with backbreaking work. It was work that Collin welcomed. The relentless motions involved in clearing debris and digging through the ugliness the fire had left behind helped deaden the ache in him just a little.

But when daylight had slipped away and the darkness outside seemed to match the bleakness of his spirit, images crept back in.

As soon as he closed his eyes the faces of his wife and

sons drifted before him. As painful as that was, he could have borne it — except for the sounds! They rose unbidden in his head; he could not push them away.

It always began the same way — the laughing shouts of his children at their chores or at play, the soft tone of Susan's words soothing him after a hard day's work.

But then it changed. It always changed. The boisterous voices of his children and the gentle voice of his wife grew distorted. They slowed down, sped up; they took on tones and tempos he had never heard from their mouths — and yet, he recognized their voices as surely as if his ears had really heard and recorded those sounds.

Over and over, Collin Haverill heard the shrieks of terror, the cries of pain and suffering, as the fire closed in around his family. The sounds chased away everything else and left him paralysed with the horror of their last moments.

Beside him, Tavish stirred and came awake. He could tell by his uncle's breathing that Collin was awake.

"Uncle?"

"Yes, Tavish?"

"Can you not sleep?"

"It's difficult," Collin said. "I'm tortured by the thought that they're gone, every one of them. And I can't help wondering ... asking God ... if He could not have spared even one of them."

"Which one?" Tavish asked. He asked it without thinking, and was horrified at the question as soon as it was out, but Collin took the question in and began to consider it.

While the moments passed, he lay on the rough floor of the crowded little house and he pondered it.

Which one?

Susan? He saw his wife's face, plump and smiling, as she went about her day's work. He thought of the warmth of her body next to him in the night and what a comfort it was to have her there when the north wind blew hard enough to bend the young birch down. He thought of her quick laugh and kind ways and he could not bring to mind anything about his wife that had disappointed him.

Adam? His oldest boy, just turned nine. He'd watched him grow, had observed with pride the strong, straight limbs of his firstborn — who was tall for his age and as limber as a sapling. Adam, who worked at his side at every opportunity, who struggled to lift things a full-grown man could hardly manage. Now and then Susan had called Adam "little Collin" and this had delighted the boy.

Kenneth? Six, and the most serious of the three — he was like a little man. The questions that boy could think of asking! Collin had recognized early that his second child was more suited to learning than labour. Kenneth was inclined to let his mind wander and he could often be found gazing off into the distance when he was supposed to be feeding the chickens or gathering tinder or performing any of the other simple chores that fell to him.

But these were not childish daydreams, and this Collin knew from the thoughts to which the boy gave voice. Already, he and Susan had begun to speak of Kenneth as their scholar and to consider, with guarded hope, what might be ahead for him.

Duncan? Even at his young age it was easy to see that the youngest member of the family was the one who was most like his mother in temperament. As an infant he had rarely cried, and of late, at two, he had toddled about as happily as any child Collin had ever seen. Duncan was bright and inquisitive, full of affection and that natural joy that so few possess.

Which one? Collin squeezed his eyes closed as though that could block out the hurt. He wiped away the sweat that had formed on his face and forehead. He tried to pray.

In another part of the room a woman groaned. Though Collin could not see her in the dark, he knew who she was by the sounds she made. Her breath was laboured, each one drawn with an effort that she hardly seemed to manage. A little girl — her daughter — slept at her side.

Both mother and child had been ill since they'd found their way to the little house, and, with no doctor or medicine, they both seemed a little worse each day.

Even if there had been a blanket to cover them, he

thought, that would have been something. But the few coverings the couple who owned the home possessed were already in use by others in just as much need.

At least the fire was kept burning. It was a little help, although the cold and wind penetrated the poorly sealed walls. Collin made his way carefully to the fireplace and added several pieces of wood before lying back down on the rough, wooden floor.

Tomorrow, he decided, he would try again to persuade Tavish to cross over to Chatham and try to find news of his family. Things were getting progressively more difficult in Newcastle. What food there had been was almost gone; sickness was at every hand with no help in sight, and the stench and decay of the dead — man and animal alike — were everywhere.

It seemed likely that they were all about to perish, but Collin believed there might be some small hope for those who made their way to Chatham.

CHAPTER SIXTEEN

Skye stood next to Stewart on the dock in Chatham, watching the boat get smaller and smaller. She managed to convince herself that she could still see her father's outline long after it had become indistinguishable, but finally she gave up and turned to her stepbrother.

"He'll be all right, won't he?"

"Sure he will," Stewart told her. "And anyway, he'll not be gone long. A few days maybe, or a week at most. You know yourself there's nothing over there to keep him."

"If Uncle Collin refuses to come back with him, though," Skye worried aloud, "it's possible that Father will send Tavish here and stay there with Collin himself."

"Mother would say that you're borrowing trouble," Stewart said. "It's a bad thing to be worried over something that might never happen at all."

"I suppose you're right," Skye said, but admitting it didn't help the lump that had grown in her throat as she watched her father disappear across the water. She tried to remind herself that Tavish would be glad to have his father there, and that if Uncle William was alive and had made his way back to Newcastle, Logan could send him to Chatham to join them.

Skye and Stewart walked back along the road toward the Chapman home, though neither of them was in a hurry to return. The house seemed increasingly small and cramped.

"Want to check on your friend?" Stewart asked. "Emily, isn't it?"

"Yes, it is, and that's a good idea," Skye said. She felt mildly embarrassed that Emily was her friend and yet Stewart had been the one to think of her. But there was so much to think about these days — like what would become of them all! She couldn't be blamed if a fevered friend slipped her mind.

When they arrived at her house, though, they were told Emily was almost recovered and might have company for a few moments.

"Skye, I don't believe I asked after your family when you were here a few days ago," Mrs. Russell said as she ushered them inside. "I am sorry — I was just so worried about Emily that I could think of nothing else at the time."

"Of course," Skye said, feeling suddenly quite grown

up. She gave a brief report of her family.

"I will pray for your brother, and for both of your uncles," Mrs. Russell promised after hearing the distressing news. "Now, here's our patient. She'll soon be up and about, I'd say."

Emily looked up with a wan smile. Her colour had not yet returned to normal, but, aside from being a little weak and pale, she was quite recovered from her recent illness. She was wrapped snugly with a deerskin.

The girls greeted each other almost shyly, and then Skye sat down next to her friend. As an afterthought, she turned toward Stewart, who stood awkwardly and seemed to be wondering why he'd come.

Stewart offered a quick "hello" and then was rescued by Mrs. Russell, who led him to the table. He seated himself on one of the benches and accepted a biscuit, which turned out to be very hard and dry. He ate it anyway. It would have been rude not to, and waste was considered sinful, even at the best of times.

"Where are the owners of this house?" Skye asked Emily after they'd caught up on each other's news. Both times she'd come there the door had been answered by Emily's mother, and the only others who were around were Emily's siblings.

"It's only an old widow and her son," Emily whispered. "She's been ill with the fever too, and has taken to her bed in the other room. Mother is caring for her. And of course, the son is working. I think he's very shy.

He hardly speaks a word when he comes in for meals, and never looks at anyone."

"And your father? Where is he?"

"Gone back to Newcastle yesterday," Emily said.

"And mine is gone today!" Skye said. "He means to see Tavish and Uncle Collin and try to bring them back with him."

"My father has gone to see Newcastle — or what is left of it — for himself, and to find out if anything remains of our home. None of us have set foot there since that terrible night, but we've heard that some houses were miraculously spared."

"There were a few," Skye said.

"Do you think perhaps ours is one of them?"

"I don't know. We didn't pass through that part of town, and it was so very dark, with the air so full of soot and ash, that it was impossible to see ahead more than a short distance."

"So, it's possible," Emily said. She smiled at the thought.

"Yes ... but," Skye said, "quite honestly, the chances aren't great. Almost everything was destroyed, with just a few homes spared.* I wouldn't want to see

---

* Of two hundred and sixty buildings in the town of Newcastle, only fourteen remained standing. Douglastown, Newcastle's neighbour to the east, fared no better, with only six of its seventy structures unharmed.

you disappointed."

"I'll try not to hope too hard," Emily said. Her smile and the hope on her face deflated.

"And then if it *is* there, it will be all the more exciting," Skye said, sorry for putting a damper on her friend's enthusiasm.

The girls chatted for a few more minutes and then Mrs. Russell told Skye that Emily needed to rest. "Of course you're welcome to come another day," she added as Skye and Stewart left.

They thanked her and made their way back to the Chapman home, where they found Mrs. Chapman sewing a piece of calico into a gown for the baby. Her hands moved with the speed and ease of practice and Skye watched as the needle darted in and out of the fabric.

"We're making some things for little Ellie-Sue to wear," Mrs. Chapman said. "Poor wee lamb has gone long enough in swaddling cloth. Hannah is knitting a fine, warm dress for her. Would you like to make a bonnet to go with it?"

Skye said "yes" eagerly. Without school or her usual routine of chores to occupy her, she was finding the days very long.

As she began to cast on stitches she happened to glance over at Hannah, who looked up just then and met her eyes. As though on cue, they exchanged a smile.

It was, at once, a simple and large thing for the two of them.

CHAPTER SEVENTEEN

Tavish knew at once, knew before a word was spoken, that the hand that came and rested on his shoulder belonged to his father.

"Son." There was a catch in Logan's throat and he stopped to clear it before trying to say anything more.

"Dad!" Tavish stood and turned toward the sound. He felt his father's strong arms clasp him and draw him into a firm hug. Tavish clenched his jaw and fought off the tears that threatened, unaware that his father was waging a similar battle.

"Is there any news of your Uncle William?" Logan asked once he could speak.

"Nothing. But men have been coming in from the woods daily."

"I pray that he may yet be found alive," Logan said.

Tavish murmured in agreement and then asked, "Skye? And Hannah?"

"Safe," Logan answered. "We were taken to Chatham the day after the fire, and Stewart made it across the same day he left you and Collin."

"So you've heard ... about Aunt Susan and the boys?"

"Yes, Stewart told us all of it. Where is Collin now?"

"Working with some of the other men. They've finished with burying the dead, though it looks as though there will soon be others." Tavish stopped speaking as he seemed to remember something. He leaned down, his hands circling the air around him until one fell on a small form to his right.

"This child's mother died the night before last, and she herself isn't well. Uncle Collin brought the little one to me that morning. I've kept her nearby and done what I could for her while the others are off doing whatever can be done out there — clearing away the rubble and looking for food. The child needs a doctor, but there's none to be had."

Logan looked down at the girl. She was dreadfully thin and was clothed only in a nightdress. Badly matted brown hair framed a nearly translucent face. "Does she eat?" he asked.

"Very little. She seems hungry enough when there's food to be had, but after a few morsels she lies back down and sleeps. I don't think she has the strength to manage more than a bite or two at a time."

"Do you know how old she is?"

"Eight, though the poor waif is so small you'd never think it. She's very timid, but I managed to get that much out of her yesterday. And she told me her name is Laura Blake and that she has two sisters and a brother, but I've no idea where the rest of her family might be. It was only her and her mother here."

"Perhaps the family was separated and the others have made their way to Chatham, as happened with us," Logan said.

"Yes, that could have happened," Tavish agreed. "If so, I hope someone comes along and claims the child soon. It might pick her spirits up to be with family."

Logan heard the heaviness and concern in his son's voice and knew that Tavish feared the little girl would die. By the sight of her, it was a legitimate worry. "She looks cold," he said.

"There's nothing to put over her," Tavish told him. "What few coverings there are have already been taken by others in no better condition."

"At least she's inside," Logan said. "There are still whole families here and there, huddled under rough shelters that hardly keep out the wind, much less the cold — and with no more than the scantest garments to cover them. They'll not survive much longer if they don't soon get help."

Tavish said nothing to this. As the days grew ever colder, he had been thinking of how it would be when the fierceness of winter came, when blizzards howled and raged and even the snuggest of homes couldn't keep the icy wind from penetrating. At such times the cold crept through walls and seemed to pierce right to their very bones.

And that was when they were warmly dressed in the daytime and covered with heavy blankets and furs at night — when their bodies were properly fuelled with plenty to eat. Tavish had begun to wonder how *any* of them would survive much longer.

"But help has been sent for," Logan said then, as though he'd read his son's mind. "Word of our situation has gone out to His Excellency, Lieutenant-Governor Douglas, and to other parts of New Brunswick, as well as Nova Scotia."

"And what can they do for us?" Tavish asked.

"That remains to be seen," Logan said simply. "But a vessel has already come with some food and clothing."

"I heard of this," Tavish said, "but we saw nothing from it."

"The need is so great everywhere," his father answered. "I'm told that its supplies were used up in a flash. But more will be on the way."

"Then I pray it gets here before this child dies for want of food and something to cover her," Tavish said, waving a hand in the direction of where the little girl lay.

As though he had cued her, Laura stirred and let out

a feeble whimper. She sat up and leaned toward Tavish, looking at him pitifully. He reached a hand toward her and, after a slight hesitation, she laid her own in it. His fingers closed around hers and the frail smallness of her fingers filled him with despair.

He felt in his heart that she would die and his helplessness to do anything about it overwhelmed him with sadness.

"I'm hungry," Laura said, her voice as tiny as her frame.

"Soon," Tavish told her. "Soon someone will come with food."

But Logan reached into the breast of his shirt and drew out a package that he'd concealed there. It held bread and pork and cheese, which Mrs. Chapman had wrapped and insisted he take with him for his son and brother. He broke off a piece of bread, into which he pressed a little cheese, and gave it to the child, placing it gently in her free hand.

Laura had eaten her bread and cheese and lain down once again by the time some of the others began to return to the little house. A few fish were brought in and these were quickly cooked and divided into small portions among those present.

Collin Haverill came in alone just as dusk was falling. Weary from a day of labouring on an empty stomach, he had almost crossed the room to where Tavish sat before Logan's presence registered with him.

The brothers hugged. It was an awkward moment and each was flooded with private thoughts that converged in the bond they'd known since childhood — when Logan had watched out for Collin, who looked up to him in turn with a kind of hero worship.

Now, the guilt of having been spared made Logan ashamed, as though he had somehow orchestrated his own family's survival at Collin's expense. It was nonsense, of course, but he felt it just the same.

For his part, Collin was torn between genuine happiness in knowing his brother's family was safe and an unwelcome anger that he could not quite define. It wasn't that he resented Logan's good fortune, exactly. Rather, a part of him wondered why his own losses had been so complete.

It was something each man would have to work through alone, for neither would ever give voice to his private thoughts and feelings.

CHAPTER EIGHTEEN

It was a little while later, in hearing his father tell Collin about Elizabet Susan (who, thanks to Mrs. Chapman, was now referred to most of the time as Ellie-Sue) that Tavish learned of the birth of his new sister.

At the unexpected news, he turned his head automatically toward his father and as he did, his heart jumped, because, for a second, he was sure that he saw the flicker of flames in the fireplace.

Similar flashes had occurred several times in the past few days. He'd be certain he'd caught a glimpse of something, only to have it disappear as quickly as it came. Tavish had begun to wonder if his mind was playing tricks on him.

He pushed those thoughts aside and concentrated on the conversation between his father and uncle. So, the baby had come on the night of the fire — a little girl. Tavish wondered how Skye had reacted to the birth of another girl in the family. Considering the long-standing resentment she'd carried toward Hannah, he didn't expect she'd been overjoyed.

But the talk between the men had moved on and Logan was telling Collin about the efforts that had been made to secure help for the devastated towns.

"Even if food and clothing enough for the winter were sent, there's still the matter of our homes. It seems a hopeless situation, with the forests burned for miles around us. How can we ever hope to rebuild? And even if we did, what would keep us here, now that our livelihood has been taken from us?"

Collin put his hand on his brother's shoulder. "Well, there's good news on that front at least," he said. "We've been finding that the damage to the wood is not as complete as one would think, given the scope of the fire. A good portion of the trees hereabout are remarkably unharmed, and the men from the lumbering parties have found that immense forests remain standing uninjured."*

"Then there's hope of rebuilding," Logan said slowly. "But surely the lumbering can't continue as before. Why, last year alone we exported over one hundred and forty thousand tonnes of timber."

"It's difficult to say at this point," Collin answered,

---

* Typically, a forest fire consumes only about one third of the vegetation in its path.

"but I don't think it's as impossible as it first appeared. Before the fire it seemed that the forests were endless — even a quarter of what we once had would be more than enough to provide a good living for generations to come."

Both men grew quiet at that, stirred by thoughts of Collin's boys. They would have been a good part of the next generation of Haverill men.

Tavish understood their silence, and his own despair widened. Of the Haverill boys, he alone was left — and what good was he to anyone? If anything, he would be a burden to his family from now on.

Logan saw the despair on his son's face. Saw it, and recognized its meaning. But he said nothing at that moment. Instead, he took Tavish outside a bit later, where he could speak to him in private.

"What you're thinking, son," he began, searching for the right words, "about your situation, that is. Well, it isn't that way."

"My situation," Tavish said, "is that I've become little more use than a baby."

"You mustn't believe that," Logan told him, but there was a want of conviction in his voice, and this was not lost on Tavish.

"It's the truth and we both know it," the boy answered. "Here I am, nearly a grown man, and I can't do anything but sit by while others carry all the burden of work."

"There's been many a harsh blow dealt these past days," Logan said. "We've been luckier than most and I tell you, I'm thankful to have my family alive. As you well know, others have not been so fortunate. I don't suppose your uncle would turn down the chance to have even one of his sons back — no matter what affliction came with him."

Tavish thought again of the day he had sat and listened to the sound of his uncle digging graves for the bodies of his wife and children. He hung his head, saying nothing.

Logan felt helpless standing there and looking at the boy. He'd always been proud of Tavish, had taken pleasure in watching him grow toward manhood. He wanted to tell his son that there was still a good future ahead for him, but the words wouldn't form — because he knew they were untrue.

Suddenly, he remembered Skye telling him to be sure to let Tavish know that Abby was safe, and that she had asked after him. That, at least, might pick up the boy's spirits.

"Your sister wanted me to give you a message," he said, slightly embarrassed. This was the talk of school children. "About Abby."

Tavish's head lifted; his face turned toward his father once again. There was a surge in his heartbeat. He hoped his face wasn't turning red.

"Skye said to be sure to let you know that Abby is

safe, and that she asked about you."

There was a flash of happiness — Logan saw it clearly — but it was gone in a second. Tavish shook his head. His fists clenched at his sides.

"What is that to me?" he asked. "There'd be no point for me to imagine I might walk out with her someday."

"You judge the young woman too quickly," Logan answered. "Your affliction may not matter to her."

"And what if it didn't? What difference would that make? I'll never have land and a home of my own. What life would I have to offer to anyone?"

"You don't know what lies ahead," Logan said. "None of us do. But you can't close yourself off from the world."

"I'm already closed off," Tavish said. "I've been cast into my own dark world, without so much as a glimpse of the one I've left."

"So, you've decided to give up, is that it?" Logan's voice had become hard and angry, though he wasn't entirely sure that the anger was meant for Tavish.

"Why not? Only a fool would try to do something that's impossible," Tavish retorted, his own anger rising and matching his father's.

"No, not a fool," Logan said. "A *man*. A man doesn't accept defeat so easily, or throw up his hands and quit. He rises to meet whatever challenge comes his way. A man has grit and determination. He finds strength when all strength is gone."

Tavish made no reply, nor did his face betray whatever was going on inside him at that moment. But Logan knew his son, and he knew that if anything would reach him, it would be this. Even as a child, Tavish had tried to be like the men around him.

"It's just such a one that I saw you becoming," Logan said, his anger gone. "And I'm counting on you now to lift your chin and face this and handle it like a man."

And just as Logan had known he would, Tavish nodded and set his jaw and determined to do what his father had asked.

CHAPTER NINETEEN

"Skye! Come see!" Stewart announced as he burst into the Chapman's kitchen. "A huge ship is coming."

Skye was only too happy to ask Hannah for permission to accompany Stewart to the river's edge. She'd spent the earlier part of the day being entertained by stories of Mr. Cullwick's past accomplishments, of which he claimed there were many. Even Mrs. Chapman's patience had grown thin when her guest indulged himself in describing his virtues.

"I'm sure we're all the better for knowing you," she'd said. "It's just a shame you're forced to spend your days here instead of being with your own kind."

"That's very kind of you, Mrs. Chapman," Cullwick answered, oblivious to any hidden meaning her words might carry. "But I find myself tolerating the inconveniences much better than I did at first. It just goes to show you how a person of character can adapt to conditions that are beneath him."

Mrs. Chapman frowned at that, though she managed to hold her tongue. Even so, Mr. Cullwick caught the look.

"My good lady," he said, "I assure you that no offence was meant to you or your home!"

Skye wondered how it would be possible to hear something so insulting and not take offence, but Cullwick, having offered the flimsy apology, continued on without a second thought for his hostess's feelings.

They were all thankful when Ellie-Sue set up a howl that silenced Cullwick for a while. Hannah took her time changing the baby's diaper and getting her ready to nurse, even though Ellie-Sue made her displeasure over the delay well known the whole while.

"It's good for her to cry a bit, and to get some exercise," Hannah had explained to Skye one day, while the baby's arms waved and her legs kicked. "Strengthens her lungs and her limbs."

Thanks to Mrs. Chapman's generosity, Hannah and Skye had made several garments, as well as a supply of diapers for the baby. The daily task of washing these usually fell to Skye and her hands were quickly becoming red and dry from the harsh soap, and from rubbing the soiled diapers across the scrubbing board until they were clean.

Somehow, Skye found she didn't mind, though there

would have been a time when she would have loathed the unpleasant chore. Ellie-Sue had captured her heart.

At the moment, though, her tiny sister was busy suckling while Hannah hummed softly. Her stepmother looked so serene that Skye almost hated to bother her by asking if she could go with Stewart to watch the ship coming in.

"Go, but don't be too long," Hannah said. "And mind the two of you come straight back here afterward."

Skye knew that the last instruction was more for Stewart's benefit than hers. She also knew he was quite likely to forget what he'd been told. Each day, as soon as he'd finished whatever chores he'd been given, Stewart tended to disappear, sometimes returning after dark. This made his mother anxious, even though he always seemed to have interesting stories to tell.

The two set off on the short walk to the water's edge, Skye hurrying to keep up with Stewart, who always seemed to move at a half run. They reached the river quickly and, after watching the ship's progress for a few moments, began to make their way toward the dock.

A crowd had already gathered by the time they got there, among them a number of people Skye recognized from Newcastle. As she did each time she came to the dock, Skye asked everyone she encountered from her former town if they had any news of Uncle William. Always, the answer was no.

She had just finished making inquiries when she heard her name called out. Turning to the sound, Skye was surprised to see Miranda Fraser, who, along with her husband, Peter, and their four children, had lived on the property adjacent to the Haverills. Skye returned her neighbour's greeting.

"I'm just waiting for my Peter," Miranda told her with a bright smile. "He should be along anytime."

"Oh? Where is he now?" Skye asked. There were no boats coming from the other side at the moment, so it was clear Miranda's husband must be coming from somewhere on the Chatham side of the river.

"There," Miranda answered, still smiling. She pointed vaguely.

That was when Skye realized that the woman's smile was a little too bright, and her eyes were not quite focused. With alarm, she saw that Miranda's hand was gesturing toward the river, even though there were no boats crossing.

Skye glanced at Stewart in alarm but his attention was wholly captured by the approaching ship.

"There he is!" Miranda said, excitement rising in her voice. She took hold of Skye's arm, clutching it tightly. "Over there — do you see him?"

Her voice was so convincing that Skye looked in spite of herself. She knew perfectly well that Peter Fraser wasn't out there, swimming toward them. Miranda had simply convinced herself that a piece of debris in the water had taken on her husband's form. Then another voice sounded.

"Here she is!"

Skye turned to the new voice and saw Jeremiah, one of Miranda's children, making his way toward them. A few steps behind was the oldest Fraser child, Heather. For a girl of eleven, her face was far too grim.

Reaching their mother, the children each took hold of a hand and, with weary sighs that suggested this was not the first time they had performed this task, they began to draw her away.

"Heather," Skye said softly, catching the girl's attention.

"Oh, Skye!" the girl answered. "I didn't see you there. We were so caught up with getting Mother ...." Her voice trailed off, but no further explanation was needed.

"And your father?" Skye asked. "Is he ...?"

"He drowned the night of the fire," Heather said sadly, confirming what Skye had already surmised. "But Mother won't believe it. She comes here to wait for him every time our backs are turned."

"We don't know if she'll ever be right again," added Jeremiah.

"I'm sure it will just take time," Skye said.

"Little Henry doesn't *have* much time," said Heather, her voice catching.

"The baby? Is he ill?"

"He's not ill, exactly, but Mother just sits about and stares and barely feeds him, no matter how much he cries."

"He's weaker every day," added Jeremiah. "He only cries some of the time now. Mostly he just whimpers and sleeps."

"I think we can help," Skye said, after only the slightest hesitation. "When you get your mother back to wherever you're staying, one of you fetch baby Henry back here to me."

CHAPTER TWENTY

Tavish felt his heart quicken as the boat moved slowly across the mighty Miramichi River. Hazy though it was, he was sure he could see the outline of land in the distance — a dark shape rising over the water.

It was happening more and more the past few days. At first there had been flashes, but now images were appearing for whole moments and then slowly fading. Just yesterday his father had materialized so clearly that Tavish could almost make out his facial features. When that image had receded into a dark haze, Tavish had to clamp his jaws together until they hurt to keep himself from crying out in protest.

It was now impossible for Tavish to stop himself from hoping — and longing — for his sight to return. Unable to push away the idea, he found himself daydreaming on the subject a good deal. Abby Munn was often a part of those daydreams.

As the land ahead of them dissolved into a dark grey blur, Tavish told himself it was just a matter of time — that his eyes were healing and he would soon be able to see as well as he ever had. He felt certain that, if this happened, he would never again take his sight for granted — not even for a single second.

His attention was drawn to his side then, as little Laura shivered and huddled closer to him. Tavish slipped an arm about her, frustrated that he had nothing to put around her frail little shoulders. The wind off the water was cold and he was chilled through himself. He couldn't imagine what it must be like for the thin child next to him, clothed in nothing but a nightdress.

He still had no idea where the other members of her family were, or if they had survived the fire. Perhaps he would be able to learn what had happened to Laura's father and her siblings when they reached Chatham.

Tavish had been resistant at the idea of leaving Newcastle for the neighbouring community. It felt like an act of betrayal, somehow, not only to his Uncle Collin, but to the hundreds of other people who, against all odds, remained on the north side of the river. It was only after his father had insisted, and that with a great deal of firmness, that he had agreed to board the boat that was crossing.

"The little one comes too, then," Tavish had said at last.

"You can't just take along anyone you like," Logan

had argued. "The home you're going to scarce has room for one more, never mind two. The Chapmans are good people, but we can't impose on them any more than we already have."

"She comes with me or I don't go," Tavish answered.

Logan took a few moments to answer. It was unlike his son to speak out against him that way, but that wasn't what troubled Logan. It was the condition of the child, whose every breath seemed likely to be her last.

What would it do to Tavish to be with her when what seemed inevitable occurred? It was clear he felt responsible for the little creature. Her death might well crush what spirit the boy had left.

In the end, it had been clear to Logan that, no matter what the outcome, he could not deny Tavish this thing, and so he agreed to send the girl with him.

Now at Tavish's side, Laura whimpered. The sound was as weak and frail as the child herself, and it was almost lost to the splash of oars in the water and the waves lapping the side of the boat.

"It's all right," Tavish told her automatically. "We'll be there soon and there will be a warm fire and a blanket for you."

Laura shivered, her lips nearly blue with the cold.

"And hot soup!" Tavish promised. "Good, hearty soup ... and bread too! You'll see. You'll be well in no time once we reach the home where my family is staying."

"If we can find a place to tie up," said the boat's owner. "There are ships just in at the docks, so we'll need to moor along the bank."

It was almost two hours later when the bedraggled pair stood outside the Chapman home and waited for an answer at the door. It was Mrs. Chapman who came and, though she tried to hide her alarm, the sight of a man and two children was far from welcome.

"Afternoon, ma'am," the man spoke. "I've been asked by this lad's father to see him and the girl to your door. I just now ferried the pair over from Newcastle."

"My father is Logan Haverill, ma'am," Tavish added, worried that they would be turned away before he could make this known.

"Oh! I see," Mrs. Chapman said. She stepped back and motioned them inside. "Then come in, come in. You too, sir. No doubt you could manage a cup of tea and a bite to eat before you're back about your business."

"Thank you just the same, but I must return at once to my boat," the man told her. He paused, as though unsure whether or not to speak further. In the end his sense of duty won out and he added, "The girl is quite ill, if you ask me, though I can't say if it's the fever or not."

"We'll see to her," Mrs. Chapman told him. She thanked him again, as did Hannah who had, by this time, joined her in the doorway.

"Tavish!" Hannah cried, drawing the young man to her. "How we've prayed for this moment!"

"Indeed we have," Mrs. Chapman agreed. "And what is the little one's name?"

"It's Laura. Laura Blake." Tavish lowered his voice. "Her mother died several days ago and no one has been able to find out where the rest of her family is."

Mrs. Chapman had already carried the girl inside and wrapped her in a warm shawl that had, until then, been about her own sturdy shoulders. She ladled scoops of thick broth from the stew that was simmering in the fireplace and brought the bowls, along with biscuits and two glasses of milk, over to the table.

Laura took tiny sips of the warm liquid from the spoon that Mrs. Chapman held to her trembling lips, for it would be a good while before the chill left her thin body.

"Here, let me help you, Tavish," Hannah said, guiding Tavish to the table. He stiffened, wanting to refuse the indignity of being fed like a baby, but the smell of the broth was so tantalizing that he swallowed his pride and went with his stepmother.

"Where are Skye and Stewart?" he asked, wishing it was his sister, rather than Hannah, guiding the food to his mouth.

"They've gone to the dock to see the ship coming in, but they ought not to be much longer," Hannah told him. "And what news do you have of your father?"

"He said to tell you that he means to stay in Newcastle for now and join the other men at the task they face."

"What task is that?" Hannah felt a stab of disappointment, but kept her voice level just the same.

"Why, clearing away the burned remains of the town and burying the dead livestock and other animals. Uncle Collin tells me they've now taken care of the human remains they've discovered, but the smell through the whole town leaves no doubt that there is much burying left to be done."

"It sounds *most* unpleasant."

Tavish turned to the sound of the new voice, surprised to hear a man speaking.

"I suppose that it is," he said, "but it has to be done."

"Yes, well," Cullwick said, "it's difficult to see the point of it. After all, there's nothing left of the town. I wouldn't think anyone would find it worth the bother."

"Not worth the *bother*?" Tavish echoed. "Newcastle is our *home*."

"It *was* your home," Cullwick corrected. "I don't mean to be unfeeling — and after all, I myself took up residence there, albeit for a short time, but Newcastle has been reduced to nothing more than a wasteland."

"You're wrong about that," Tavish said, unable to keep the anger from his voice. "The men who are there even now, doing the work that *every* able-bodied man should be lending himself to, have found reason to believe that Newcastle can be rebuilt."

"Rebuilt?" Hannah said. "But how?"

Cullwick gave her a disapproving look. These settler women were so crass and unrefined; had Mrs. Haverill no idea how inappropriate it was for her to interrupt a conversation of this sort — between two *men*?

But Hannah, if she was aware of Mr. Cullwick's silent reproof, paid no attention to it. Instead, she listened with rising hope as Tavish told them what had been discovered: it seemed there were trees enough surviving in the forests for Newcastle to be entirely recreated.

"*And*," he went on, "enough that the lumbering industry may well resume in the very near future."

"Even if that were true," Cullwick scoffed, "there will be no one left to rebuild. Those who once inhabited the ill-fated town will have entirely dispersed long before the spring comes, and anyone who attempts to stay will most certainly perish from cold and hunger."

CHAPTER TWENTY-ONE

Stewart was astonished, when he returned to Skye's side after a short exploration along the water's edge, to find her holding an infant.

"What have you got there?" he asked, staring at the tiny form in her arms.

"A baby."

"Yes, I can see that. But *why* do you have a baby?"

"This is Henry, the youngest child of Peter and Miranda Fraser, our neighbours," Skye said. "It seems that Peter drowned on the night of the fire and Miranda is ... unwell, and cannot feed the little one."

"But why *you* have him?" Stewart asked again.

"Someone has to take care of him until his mother is well again," Skye said.

"Well, sure," Stewart said, "but why *us*? We already have a crying baby in the house."

Skye smiled. "Then what's one more?"

Stewart shrugged, his interest in the matter already fading. He turned back to face the water as the ship got ever nearer.

"It's called the *Orestes*," he announced to Skye, as though she couldn't see the name for herself. "And look! There are some other, smaller vessels coming not far behind."

Skye glanced toward the great ship, noting the others in the distance, but her interest in their arrival had dimmed greatly. Rather, the listless baby Henry had captured her attention.

"I think I'd better go back to the house," she told Stewart. "This child needs care — and right away — if he's to have a chance at all."

"I suppose I'd best go with you," Stewart said with a sigh. "Mother won't be very happy if I don't walk you back."

"There's no need of that. I know my way perfectly well by now."

"Are you sure? I don't mind, really."

"Honestly, I'll be fine." Skye set off while Stewart once again fixed his eyes on the activity on the water. Choosing to go along the road rather than the river, she made her way quickly toward the Chapman house.

Once she had nearly reached it, though, her steps slowed and faltered. What had she been thinking, offering to take this baby home with her without even asking Hannah or Mrs. Chapman if it would be all right?

The house wasn't hers to invite another mouth into, nor would the job of feeding him fall to her.

And so, it was with some anxiety that she stepped through the kitchen door, steeling herself for the reactions to her rash decision.

"Tavish!" she cried, seeing her brother there. Tavish stood and turned to face the sound of his sister's voice as she continued. "When did you come? And how did you get here? I've just come from the dock. How did you pass by Stewart and me unnoticed?"

"Our boatman tied up downstream of the dock. We got here just a short time ago," Tavish said.

"So Father is with you?"

"No ... he stayed behind with Uncle Collin."

"But you said 'we.'" Skye looked past Tavish then and, even before he spoke, saw the small girl seated near the fireplace.

"Yes, I did," Tavish acknowledged. He explained about Laura Blake, who darted a glance at Skye and then looked away just as quickly.

"Skye?" Hannah lifted Ellie-Sue to her shoulder and gently patted her back.

"Yes?"

"You have a *baby* with you," Hannah pointed out.

"Oh! Yes. But I can explain." Skye said. Glancing back and forth from Hannah to Mrs. Chapman as she spoke, Skye gave details of how little Henry had come to be in her arms.

"He needs a wet nurse," Skye ended. "And I didn't know what else to do but bring him here, though I know I had no right to impose further on the kindness and hospitality we've known in this home."

"A wet nurse," Hannah echoed.

"Another baby!" Mr. Cullwick groaned.

"I didn't know what else to do," Skye repeated helplessly. "I'm sorry."

"Don't be silly, child." Mrs. Chapman stepped forward and took baby Henry from the girl's arms. "You did just right."

"What is this — an *orphanage*?" Cullwick grumbled. "Is every child who's gone for more than a few hours without a meal to be brought here?"

"Oh, hush!" Mrs. Chapman said.

Hannah and Skye both looked at their hostess in surprise, but it was Cullwick who was the most astonished. His mouth fell slack and red crept up his neck and across his dumbfounded face.

"Were you addressing *me*, madam?" he asked when he could find his voice.

"Indeed I was, Mr. Cullwick. Since your arrival here you've insulted my husband, my home, my other guests, and myself. While others have struggled with great difficulties and trials, you've been more concerned with your own imagined sufferings, which, quite frankly, all combined aren't worth mentioning."

Cullwick's jaw had gone slack once more and Skye

might have laughed at the sight of him sitting with his mouth gaping open — but for the fact that it was more pathetic than amusing.

Mrs. Chapman's tone softened. "I'm truly sorry to have to speak to you in this manner, Mr. Cullwick, but I believe I've held my tongue long enough. You're welcome in this home, but I must ask that henceforth you keep your complaints to yourself. We've enough to contend with without your disagreeable narrative."

Cullwick managed to make his jaw cooperate at last and his mouth snapped closed. He cleared his throat several times before speaking.

"Madam, I beg you to believe that I am mortified to learn of your feelings, and to discover that I have offended you. I assure you that that was never my intention. Please accept my most humble apology."

Skye doubted that Cullwick was honestly capable of humility, but Mrs. Chapman gave him a nod and a thin smile before turning her attention back to little Henry.

"Well, now, little fellow," she said. "It looks as though you've come to us just in time."

CHAPTER TWENTY-TWO

Tavish and Stewart were among the crowd that gathered to hear His Excellency, Lieutenant-Governor Sir Howard Douglas on October 27. They, like the other inhabitants of Miramichi, were astonished by the arrival of their beloved governor at noon that Thursday.

It was easy for the two boys to feel the joy and gratitude that rose from the townsfolk as they greeted Douglas. That their esteemed governor would leave the seat of parliament at such a time of year, when his own community had also been affected by the fire (although to a much lesser degree) and would travel so many miles to visit them in their time of need, touched the hearts of the sufferers as nothing else could do.

Douglas spoke with great compassion to the people of the area. He assured them of his desire to comfort and console them and of his commitment to seeing that every possible effort would be made to assist them and to restore their towns.

The boys reported the details later that day when he'd returned to the Chapman home.

"It was the first time I've felt any real hope about our situation since the night of the fire," Stewart said, speaking in a more subdued manner than usual. "His Excellency told us that we mustn't give up and quit the place, but that if we hold together and be strong we can triumph over the hard times that lie ahead. I felt, in that moment, that no hardship was too great to overcome."

"The whole crowd felt the same way," Tavish added, "I could hear it in the voices around me — how those things that no one would have thought could be done suddenly seemed possible."

"And when he'd finished his speech," Stewart said, "he spent time talking with groups of poor and homeless people."

"What do you think of that, Laura?" Tavish asked, trying to jolly the girl a little. "His Excellency came all the way here just to see us!"

The only response from Laura, however, was a fit of coughing. Skye and Mrs. Chapman tended to her as the room echoed with the deep, hollow sounds that seemed too large to have come from so tiny a frame. By and by the eruption subsided and the sickly child drifted into an exhausted sleep.

Tavish felt a surge of frustration that he had been

unable to help as he listened and peered at the grey blurs before him. Though he was now quite certain that his eyes were slowly improving, there was still very little definition in the shadowy figures that moved through his field of vision. It remained to be seen whether or not his sight would fully return, or whether he would spend his life squinting at ghostly outlines.

Mrs. Chapman held Laura, who was wrapped snugly in a blanket that had been sacrificed from the woman's own bed. She rocked her gently in her arms, fighting tears as she looked down at the pale, sleeping face. Even the child's lips were without colour.

Mr. Chapman stood, cleared his throat awkwardly and spoke. The room grew instantly hushed as the normally quiet man spoke.

"This little girl needs our prayers," he said simply. Then he nodded and sat down again.

As though he had issued a command, every head bowed and every heart lifted up a prayer for little Laura Blake.

In the corner where he was so often seated, Dalton Cullwick offered the first genuine prayer of his life, one that was in no way meant to benefit himself.

CHAPTER TWENTY-THREE

For the Haverills, as for so many Miramichiers, it was the deciding factor. Certainly, Lieutenant-Governor Douglas's visit to the Miramichi towns following the Great Fire would be spoken of for years to come. The entire community was moved by the fact that their beloved governor would make the journey in order to bring hope and comfort to the townsfolk — that he would walk among the ruins of Douglastown and Newcastle in order to be certain that he fully understood the devastation caused by the inferno.

When he was satisfied that he had done all that was possible for the moment, Douglas returned to Fredericton by proceeding up the river in a birch canoe.

He left behind a people with renewed vigour and determination, a people who would face the days ahead with more courage than they had believed themselves to possess. The hardships they faced were many, but they rose to each occasion and pressed forward.

Looking back at the weeks immediately following the fire, Skye Haverill wondered that she had thought them such a trial. So she *wasn't* in her own home ... so what? The crowded atmosphere of the Chapman house, the annoyance of Mr. Cullwick and his arrogance — these things soon appeared to her as inconveniences so minor they were not worth mentioning.

She would always remember the date that everything changed for the worse. It was November 19, the day after she and Stewart had stood on the dock with so many others, waving goodbye to Captain Litchfield and his crew as the *Orestes* parted water and began its journey back to Halifax.

Skye had been sitting near the fire and holding little Henry, who, after only a few weeks in their care, had almost entirely recovered both his appetite and spirit. He was a good baby, gurgling and cooing happily most of the time, in contrast to Ellie-Sue, who cried a great deal.

Skye had just been thinking that it would be nice if Ellie-Sue's temperament were a bit more like Henry's, then feeling guilty for what seemed disloyalty to her sister, when Logan Haverill stepped through the door.

"Papa!" she cried, jumping to her feet and startling Henry who, taking her sudden movement as some sort of game, laughed in excitement.

Logan started toward her but stopped suddenly, staring in bewilderment at the baby in her arms. This brought laughter from both Hannah and Mrs. Chapman. The ladies realized at once that his confusion was because he'd thought the child was Ellie-Sue, who was considerably smaller and had dark hair in comparison to Henry's fine blonde fuzz.

Hannah's smile faded, though, as she told her husband the sad news of Peter Fraser, and his wife's reaction to the tragedy.

"Peter Fraser," Logan said with a shake of his head. "A terrible loss to his family — *and* the community. Peter was a good Christian man. I never knew him to turn away anyone who went to him for help, and you couldn't ask for a better neighbour."

Skye looked down at Henry, remembering how her heart had sunk when she'd first held his limp body in her arms. She had scarcely dared breathe as she'd carried him to the Chapmans' home that day, so frightened was she that he would die on the way.

And now, here he was, cooing happily, waving his fists about while his bright eyes darted here and there. All at once, Skye's eyes filled with tears and she turned quickly away from the others.

What is *wrong* with me, she wondered, confused by the sudden rush of emotion. As though he was just as puzzled as she by the whole thing, Henry's eyes widened and he put several fingers to his mouth, looking very much as if he were giving the matter some serious thought.

"Skye?"

Skye wiped away her tears and cleared her throat as she turned to once again face her father.

"Did you hear what I said?"

"No," she admitted.

"Your Uncle Collin and I, as well as Stewart, will spend the winter months in Newcastle. We've been preparing the root cellar of our house so that we can continue with any reconstruction and other work that's possible."

No one noticed Tavish flinch at his father's words. It galled him that Stewart, who was several years his junior, had been included while he was not mentioned. Of course, why would he be? he thought bitterly. He could be of no use to them.

"Preparing the root cellar?" Skye repeated, stunned at the implication. His words *couldn't* mean what she thought they meant.

"Yes." Logan took a deep breath and confirmed the unthinkable. "To live in through the winter."

"What? Live in the root cellar?!" Hannah echoed. "Impossible!"

"We'll not be the only ones," Logan told them. "Lots of folk are doing the same. It's the only solution."

"Well, now, of course you're all welcome to stay here until winter passes," Mrs. Chapman said.

"You and your husband have been more than kind," Logan told her. "I pray the Good Lord will bless you for all you've done but there are too many of us, and the job ahead is too great to wait for spring."

"We do need to impose on your hospitality a while longer yet," he continued, "for the cellar is dark and cramped and the poorest form of shelter. With your kind permission, Hannah and the baby and Tavish will remain behind for the time being. And these other two children, of course," he added, nodding toward Henry and Laura.

"And me!" Skye added, pointing out what she believed to be an oversight.

"I'm afraid you'll be needed with us," Logan said.

Skye stared in disbelief, unable to fully take in what she'd just heard. Surely, he couldn't mean it!

It pained Logan to see his daughter's distress, even though he knew there was no way around it. "I'm sorry, Skye," he said gently, "but we don't have a choice. You're needed there to tend to the fire and make the meals."

While Skye struggled to accept her father's words, Tavish fought the anger that was building inside him. He tried to remember what Logan had told him about facing and handling his situation, but a single word crowded out everything else:

Useless!

CHAPTER TWENTY-FOUR

Skye blinked several times and then closed her eyes, opening them slowly as they adjusted to the bright glare of the outside world. She couldn't remember it ever being quite this bright before, with light bursting everywhere as the snow reflected the sun's radiance.

Those first few moments outside were almost painful these days, so accustomed had she become to the damp and murky atmosphere of the cellar. Some days the only times she emerged were for quick trips to the outhouse. Even then, as she squinted her way along she felt as though she understood what it must be like to be a mole, scurrying about blindly.

But this was Sunday, and they were going to the worship service that Reverend Webber had organized. It was only the second one that the Haverills had been able to attend, since the location had to be rotated from week to week. The loss of their buggies, sleighs, and many of their horses made travel difficult enough, and the snow and cold did nothing to improve the matter.

Today, it was but a few miles to the house where the service was to be held, and so they were able to travel on foot — Logan and Collin Haverill out in front, Skye and Stewart moving along steadily behind them.

It felt good to Skye, breathing in the crisp, clean air of the outdoors after so much time stuck in the gloom of the cellar. She inhaled deeply as she walked along while her eyes drank in the glistening white of the snow that blanketed the landscape, and the bright blue sky overhead.

If only spring would come early, she thought. The winter had been so long already, and there were likely to be several more months of snow and cold — months of being trapped in the earth. Sometimes, when the thought hit her that they were living in a hole in the ground — a hole that had been dug to house vegetables — Skye felt that this must all be a terrible dream and that she would surely wake to find things just as they once were.

The lovely scent of fresh air was like an elixir to her after enduring the heavy, sour smell of the cellar. Lingering scents of burned and rotted vegetables mixed with the smells of body odour, dank earth, and the ever-present thin haze of smoke that escaped the chimney's draw and seeped quite steadily from the makeshift fireplace. And though Skye kept the fire going as best she could, it was no match for the permeating damp.

Why, even the bannock she made grew limp and tacky before long.

Skye was also tired of cooking the same things over and over! Mush, salt pork, and potatoes and bannock day after day. No one complained, of course — it was the same for everyone — but Skye found herself daydreaming about carrots and turnip, apples and berries.

Soon, she thought, as she crunched along on the snow's packed surface, spring would be there. Soon, the house would be rebuilt and life would return to normal. Best of all, she would be let out of the prison that had been her home since the day they'd returned to Newcastle.

Skye longed for the warm breezes of summer, the freedom of running through open fields and the spurting greens of blades and buds — the start of new life growing. She longed for a long hot bath and the friendly stiffness of freshly laundered clothes against her skin. Her scalp itched constantly, and she could hardly wait to be able to wash her hair properly again. It was challenging enough to attend to one's hygiene through a normal winter, but this year had been worse than any other.

As they often did, Skye's thoughts drifted to Tavish and Hannah and Ellie-Sue, as well as the Chapmans and little Laura and baby Henry. (She wasted no time wondering about Mr. Cullwick!) It was hard not to feel envious of them, living with the comforts of a normal home while she crept about in her dirt hovel.

Skye tried not to think too much about Uncle William and what his fate must have been. It seemed foolish to hold onto hope when it was almost certain William would have made his way to them long before now ... if he had survived.

The sound of someone calling her name drew Skye's attention back to the moment and when she turned she saw Emily Russell and her family coming along the trodden path.

Skye had been surprised to see the Russells at the last Sunday service they'd attended, but she had soon learned that Emily's family was also living in *their* cellar. The girls had shared hurried bits of news after the sermon, but there was scarcely time to catch up on the basics before their families left once again for their homes.

Skye waved vigorously, gesturing for Emily to hurry and catch up to her. Before long the two had their heads together.

"I don't know how I can bear this much longer," Emily lamented. "Most days it's too cold to take the little ones out and then they whine the whole day long. 'It's too dark. We can't play! Why must we eat the same food every day?' I slapped Louise the other day just because she wouldn't stop, and of course Mother was frightfully cross at me over that. But what was I to do? I felt if I had to listen to Louise's complaining for one more minute I might do something desperate."

"I suppose that would be trying enough, all right,"

Skye said. "Still, after months of being alone day after day, I'd welcome the sound of any voice, even a whining child."

"I hadn't thought of that," Emily admitted. "It must be horrible, being by yourself most of the time — and with so little light. I think that's the worst thing for me."

"I hate it, too," Skye agreed. "Some days it feels as though the darkness is creeping closer and closer — as if its shadows are about to swallow up even the bit of light from the fire. I never saw such thick, heavy shadows before."

"If only candles weren't so scarce," Emily said.

"It's the *sun* I miss," Skye told her. She turned her face heavenward, basking in the bright rays. "I can hardly wait for spring!"

"Just a few more months," Emily said, her voice wistful.

The girls fell silent then, for they'd reached the home where the church service was to be held — one of the few structures that had survived the fire. They went inside, each with her own family, and found places on the rough, makeshift benches that had been made for these small assemblies.

Reverend Webber looked out over the tiny congregation that had come together there that morning, and as he bowed his head to pray, it struck him that these little gatherings were more than worship services.

The little group that was present somehow seemed to represent all that had been lost. Homeless, reduced in a single night from prosperity to poverty, there they were, heads bowed before God.

And yet, at the same time, there was an air of hope and trust among them, and it seemed to Reverend Webber that this feeling was not spiritual alone.

Rather, it was as though they had formed, even in their diminished state, a new community, bonded together in hardship in a way that they had never known when they had been favoured with good fortune.

CHAPTER TWENTY-FIVE

Skye thought later that it was lucky her father hadn't taken the letter from his pocket until the men were heading back out after the noonday meal. He handed it to her as he began the ascent to the ground.

"This just arrived, but I'm not sure what to do with it. Put it somewhere safe for now, would you, Skye?"

A shock ran through Skye as she stared at Uncle William's name on the front. Seeing it there so unexpectedly brought up a sudden wave of grief and she found that she was unable to keep from weeping.

So, Charlott Willoughby had decided to write, just as Uncle William had guessed she would.

Skye wondered what the letter said, and whether its contents would have been welcome news to her uncle. If only she could get a peek inside ...

She inspected the wax seal on the back of the folded sheet, but went no further. It would be wrong to read someone else's personal correspondence, even if the seal had been missing altogether.

Over the next few days she struggled with what to do about the letter. Of course, she meant to keep her word to Uncle William and write back to Charlott. The problem lay in knowing what to write.

Do I tell her he was lost in the fire? she wondered. Or should I say simply that he is missing? How horrible would it be to this girl, who Skye had heard profess her love for William, to hear either bit of news? Would it be kinder to let some time pass? Would she be better prepared for the worst if a reply were very slow in coming?

In the end, she was compelled to wait for want of paper, which she had some difficulty obtaining. Nearly two weeks passed, during which time she composed the letter in her head almost every day as she prepared meals, did what cleaning was possible, and stoked the fire.

When she finally secured a sheet of paper and made a small bottle of ink, Skye wondered what had happened to all of the fine phrases and careful words she'd thought of. Her head was blank and every opening line that occurred to her seemed cold or trite or too-familiar. It was so hard to find the right balance writing, as it were, to a stranger.

While Skye knew who Charlott was, she felt it unlikely that the same was true the other way around. Finally, after much deliberation, she wrote the following:

Newcastle, Thursday, March 2, 1826

Dear Miss Willoughby;

I regret to tell you that your letter, addressed to my uncle, Mr. William English, has not reached him. It is my unhappy duty to inform you that my uncle's whereabouts have been unknown since the dreadful conflagration that swept through the area last October 7. While we continue to hope, the worst is feared.

Your letter waits here unopened and will remain so until you are able to send instructions for it.

Sincerely yours,
Skye Haverill

Skye read the letter over several times before folding it carefully and then sealing it closed by dripping her candle over the back flap. She compared the two letters, one sealed with red sealing wax and stamped with the initial C, the other held closed by a rather uneven blob of candle wax. Skye couldn't help thinking that what she had written was probably just as lacking in comparison to the letter Charlott Willoughby had sent.

Oh, what does it matter? she asked herself as a well of

sorrow rose up in her. She could picture Uncle William's face and the yearning she'd seen on it as he'd talked to Charlott only a few months before. Many tears fell as she went about her tasks that day.

It was several days before Skye had an opportunity to send the letter off to Charlott. She wondered how long it would take for it to reach England, and when she might expect a reply.

She needn't have worried about that, however, for less than a week after Skye had sent the off the letter, Uncle William's fate was discovered.

It was mid afternoon, a bright, cold day. Skye was carrying water, and so she was walking a little slower than normal along the path back to her cellar. She breathed in deeply as she walked, happy to fill her lungs with the sweet, fresh outdoor air.

To her surprise, Skye saw Stewart and her father coming toward her, even though it was too early for them to be stopping work for the evening meal. Shielding her eyes from the sun's glare, Skye saw, though they were still quite distant, that there was something odd about her father's gait.

Is Papa limping? she wondered. Perhaps the ground is just uneven, or maybe he's carrying something heavy. But she couldn't see him holding anything, and Stewart seemed to be walking quite normally, so it couldn't be the ground.

I hope he hasn't injured himself, Skye thought.

It was so easy for wounds to get red and swollen. She experienced a wave of fear as she remembered how a classmate's father had taken ill and died from what had begun as a simple cut.

And then, in a flash, she realized that her father wasn't limping at all, for the man with Stewart was *not* Logan Haverill.

It was William English.

CHAPTER TWENTY-SIX

"*U*ncle *William*!" Skye cried. She nearly spilled the water in her haste to sit it down and run along the path toward the duo. "Uncle William, is it really you?"

"It is," William said. He grinned and opened his arms as Skye flew into them.

"I thought we would never see you again!" Skye said, barely able to get the words out between sobs of joy.

"I thought I was a goner myself," William told her. "And I would be too, but for a group of Mi'kmaqs finding me. But come, I've been dreaming of a cup of tea for days. Put one in my hand and I'll gladly tell you the whole story."

Stewart took over carrying the water and the threesome made their way to the cellar and climbed down into it. Within a few moments Skye had placed the coveted tea, along with bannock and a ladle of oatmeal, before her uncle.

As he ate, William explained how, on the night of the fire, he'd been struck and injured by a burning tree as the men fled from the camp to a deep brook nearby. By sheer strength of will, he had managed to reach the water in time to escape the full blaze. But he found himself alone there. His companions, thinking him lost in the inferno, had made their way further along to a wider place in the brook.

Late the following day, William had dragged himself to a spot on the bank. Injured and alone, he knew that there was little chance for him to make it out of the woods alive. He couldn't walk, and dragging himself so many miles would be impossible.

It was on the third day, when fever had set in and death seemed near, that he felt himself being lifted and carried away. Much of the next weeks seemed a dream, hands bathing him, liquids held to his lips. Drifting in and out of consciousness, William finally saw that he was in the hands of a small group of Mi'kmaqs.

His recovery had been slow, and the process of rebuilding the strength in his leg long and painful. At last, when he was well enough to travel, snow and cold prevented him. And so, he had passed the last months gaining strength and thinking.

"Thinking?" Skye echoed as William reached the end of his story.

"Yes. Wondering why I was spared. Feeling that there must be some greater purpose for my life." William paused and then reached for his niece's hand. "You two will be the first to hear this. I've had a call."

"A call?" Stewart repeated.

"To serve the Lord. As a preacher."

Skye was too astonished to speak. Uncle William had never seemed particularly religious, although he attended services with the family whenever he was there. Picturing him at the front of a church giving a sermon like Pastor Webber almost made her giggle, except that she could see how serious he was.

The thought came to her that Charlott Willoughby would be just as astounded by this news, which made her jump up from the table so suddenly that Uncle William almost dropped his tea.

"Oh!" she said. "A letter came for you, just as you thought it might. I've sent off a message as you'd asked, though I confess I didn't give very cheerful news."

Uncle William's face had gone very still.

"You didn't say he was dead or anything like that, did you?" Stewart asked.

"No, of course not!"

"That's a good thing, since I'm not." William laughed, regaining his composure. He looked questioningly at Skye and said, "So, this letter ...?"

"Goodness! Of course! It's right here." Skye hurried to the side of the room and retrieved the letter from the makeshift shelf where she'd placed it for safekeeping.

"I don't know that I can read it in this poor light,"

William said as he looked down at the fine script that bore his name.

Skye fetched a candle and lit it for him, then forced herself to sit on the other side of the room. She even managed not to stare, though she couldn't help stealing a few glances as her uncle read.

It was difficult to interpret his expression while he was reading, but when he'd finished he lifted his head and a smile slowly spread itself across his face.

"There's good news?" Skye asked eagerly and then, remembering that she wasn't supposed to know anything about the situation, quickly added, "From your friend?"

"Well, now, that depends," William answered.

Skye wished that Stewart wasn't there just then. If he hadn't been, she was quite sure she'd have gathered the nerve to tell Uncle William what she'd seen that day the August before. And then, as though he'd read her mind, Stewart stood and stretched.

"I might as well bring some wood down for the fireplace," he said, "since I'm missing part of the afternoon's work with the men."

As soon as Stewart had climbed up and out of the cellar, and before she could lose her nerve, Skye plunked herself down beside her uncle and told him of how she'd been gathering berries and had witnessed the exchange between him and Charlott Willoughby.

"I truly didn't *mean* to spy on you!" she ended after rushing through the story.

"I know you didn't," he said at once. "And there's no harm done in any case."

"And the letter from Miss Willoughby," Skye could scarcely believe her nerve, "I saw that it made you smile."

William laughed and reached over to pat Skye on the hand. "I'd almost think you'd like to know what was in this letter," he chuckled. "It must have been a kind of torture for you to have it here and not be able to see what it said."

"It was!" Skye admitted, which made William laugh again.

"But can I trust you to keep a secret?"

"Oh, yes! I've not said a single word to anyone about you and Miss Willoughby, and I've known since last summer!"

William spread the letter open again and looked down at it, as though he needed to see the words once more to be sure he'd not imagined them.

"Charlott will be returning home this coming summer, and means to stand up to her father and insist on having her own choice for a husband."

"You!" Skye squealed.

William smiled. But inside, something was already troubling him.

CHAPTER TWENTY-SEVEN

Staying at the Chapmans' home that winter was more difficult for Tavish than anyone could begin to imagine. While everyone around him tried to be compassionate and understanding, all Tavish felt was pitied. What he *wanted* was to feel useful again. Special treatment only infuriated him, though he had enough maturity to hide this. He might well have fallen into a state of despair but for the fact that Fay Chapman decided that something needed to be done to help the boy.

Her plan was simple, yet effective. Most importantly, it was clever enough that Tavish didn't see through it. What Mrs. Chapman did was distract Tavish from his problems by occupying him with a wide variety of tasks both inside and outside the house. And, by keeping him busy, she accomplished something far more important, for Tavish began to realize that he was not nearly as handicapped as he had supposed.

He quickly learned that there was much he could do by feel and even more by simply not giving up. By repeating his efforts again and again, he found he could achieve almost any task he'd been given. And then the repetition became less and less until he could often do something on the first or second try that might have needed twenty or thirty tries to manage before.

With each success, Tavish felt his spirits lifting. He came to understand that, blind or sighted, there were things he could do, and he began to believe that it *was* possible for him to have a future either way. And all the while that his spirit was being mended, another miracle of healing was taking place.

It had been happening so gradually, and he had been so busy concentrating on the duties assigned to him by Mrs. Chapman, that it was several days before Tavish really recognized the significance of what was before him: not merely shadows and shades, but actual forms and shapes. They were hazy, but were defined enough that he could almost identify them.

Once he realized it, of course, he strained to distinguish whatever was before him, which only caused his head to hurt and the vague outlines to fade and blur. But when he relaxed, well, that was different. Before long he could quite easily identify pieces of furniture, and within weeks of that he found that he could even tell one person from another by the shadows that defined their facial features.

Day by day his sight improved. There was greater clarity and more distinct colour and Tavish gave thanks for each small bit of progress.

By the time winter was loosening its grip on the community, he could see well enough to get about without any real difficulty and was able to function on a fairly normal level.

What a joy it was to be able to do man's work again! Even so, Tavish felt guilty when he told Mrs. Chapman that she would henceforth have to manage without his help, for he knew she had come to rely on him for many tasks.

"Don't you worry your head about it," she said, hiding a smile. Good thing the boy didn't realize she'd often had to wrack her brain to come up with something for him to do. "We managed before and we'll manage again. I'm just glad your sight is coming back — that's what really matters."

Tavish had made the transition to working outside with Mr. Chapman without any real problem. He was more annoyed than surprised to find his muscles stiff and sore after the first few days, but this worked itself out quickly as he became re-accustomed to the heavier labour.

Being outdoors was so much better than spending his days inside with the womenfolk — and Mr. Cullwick. Tavish found it odd that Cullwick could seem so content to stay inside, and to do nothing, day after day. The man was somehow able to ignore every hint that suggested he might make himself useful in some manner, and the only times he ventured out were for Sunday service or to seek out books or tobacco or some other item that he felt would make his life more pleasant.

As the weather grew ever milder, Tavish often found Laura Blake peeking shyly around a corner as he worked. If the job at hand posed no threat to her, he would call her over and talk to her, but she seldom contributed to the conversations. Rarely, she might smile at something he said, and this was as much reaction as he might expect in a whole afternoon.

And then they came for her. It was late afternoon when the carriage pulled up and a man and woman stepped out. He was quite short and rather stocky, while she stood a good head taller and was dreadfully thin.

"Hello, then!" spoke the man, spying Tavish. "This is the Chapman home then, is it?"

"Yes."

"And there's a little Blake girl here? Laura, I think's her name."

"Yes." Tavish felt something turn cold inside him.

"Well then, you'll be glad to know we're her kin, come to take her off your hands. We'd have come before now, but we thought they were all dead, didn't we Bella?"

Bella managed to nod her head without looking the least bit interested in the subject.

"Well, there you have it." The man smiled, showing decaying teeth.

"I'm Tavish Haverill," Tavish said, regaining his wits and stepping forward to offer his hand. "Some of my family are staying with the Chapmans."

"Lyman McLean," the man said as he shook Tavish's hand. "And this here's my wife, Bella. She and the Blake girl's mother were sisters."

"I'm so sorry for your loss, ma'am," Tavish said at once.

"It was a terrible blow to me," Bella McLean sniffed. "And me with seven of my own to raise, about to be saddled with another."

"It's our duty," her husband reminded her, patting her arm. "After all, the child can't be left with nowhere to go. And anyway, she's near old enough to give you some help with the little ones. Just the right age to be trained proper for the job, in fact."

He turned to Tavish again and said, "Now, if you'll lead the way, my boy, we'll take her off these good people's hands."

With his heart sinking, Tavish showed them to the house and introduced them to Mrs. Chapman. It was clear that they had no real interest in Laura and that they meant only to make her a sort of unpaid servant. But they were family, so objecting would be useless.

Inside the house, Mrs. Chapman made a swift assessment of the situation and came to the same conclusions that Tavish had reached. Smiling to hide her uneasiness, she insisted on setting out some biscuits and tea for the McLeans, and told Tavish to run and fetch Mr. Chapman so that he could say goodbye to Laura.

Tavish did as he was asked, but found himself telling Mr. Chapman of his misgivings about Laura's aunt and uncle.

"They don't seem to really care about her," he said angrily. "And after all she's been through!"

Mr. Chapman was as quiet as usual. Even so, Tavish knew the thought of Laura being taken away under such circumstances did not sit well with him.

A second round of introductions was made when Nathan Chapman entered the house, but the McLeans clearly had no interest in lingering. Laura was at their side by then, looking frightened and quite miserable as she realized she was to be taken away by these people.

"Well, Laura," Mrs. Chapman said, squatting down in front of her, "it looks as though you're to be leaving with your aunt and uncle here. I suppose you're glad to see them again, aren't you?"

Laura tried to force a smile, but her mouth trembled and, after a few seconds, she gave up and began to cry softly, tears spilling down over her pale cheeks.

"Now, now, there's no need of that," Lyman McLean said crossly. "She mayn't remember us, but she needn't go on that way."

"She's a little girl," Mrs. Chapman said. Her voice

was barely audible.

"A spoiled one at that." Bella sniffed. "We'll teach her that performances such as this won't do her any good. Not one of our seven would act this way, you can be sure of that!"

"We may have indulged her a little," Fay Chapman said, "but she's been through so very much."

"You say that you've got seven already?" Mr. Chapman asked.

"We have, and all raised to do as they're told!"

"Taking on another could well be a burden," Mr. Chapman said.

"Oh, it will, it will. But we know our duty," Lyman answered.

"Well, you know, she could stay here. We've room and, quite frankly, we've grown fond of her."

Mrs. Chapman's face lit up with hope at her husband's words, but the glimmer was quickly extinguished.

"And what do you take us for?" Lyman demanded angrily. "Do you mean to suggest that we're the kind of people who would go about giving away our kin?"

"Of course he doesn't. That's not what he was saying at all."

Every head turned toward the corner where Mr. Cullwick sat in his usual place near the fire.

"No one meant for you to *give* her away," he continued. "Of course, you'd be fairly compensated for your loss."

The McLeans were stunned into silence. Though both would have liked to claim they were offended by such an appalling suggestion, those sentiments were overridden by greed.

"I happen to have recently received a yearly disbursement from my late uncle's estate," Cullwick went on. "Now, what would you say might be a fair sum for this child's services from now until she reaches adulthood?"

Lyman McLean's face had grown very red. He stammered and cleared his throat before stating a price. It was an outrageous amount.

"Done," said Cullwick without batting an eye. He drew forth a sheet of parchment and wrote out a brief agreement, which both McLeans signed. When this was done, he pulled a pouch from an inner pocket, counted out the agreed-upon price, and passed it into Lyman McLean's trembling hand.

When the couple had gone (without so much as saying goodbye to Laura!) the Chapmans were profuse with their thanks and tried to insist that they would repay the sum.

"Nonsense! I won't entertain such an idea," Cullwick told them. "I'm happy for the chance to return some of the kindness you've shown these past months. But come now, let us speak of it no more, for you surely know by now that I am a modest and humble man."

"Whatever else you may be," Tavish said, "you're a good and decent man."

And he meant it, though until that very day he'd never have guessed he could ever possess such an opinion of Dalton Cullwick.

CHAPTER TWENTY-EIGHT

Skye laughed in delight at the antics of a squirrel that was racing about and chattering angrily at her. It was obvious from the way it was behaving — with sudden back-and-forth jumps in her direction — that it had young nearby and was trying to frighten her off.

"You're not that scary," she told it after one particularly fierce burst of nattering and aggressive leaps. Then, taking pity on it, she moved away a little while she continued with the chore of washing clothes.

It was *so* good to be able to launder things again! The first thing she'd had to do when her father had found the cauldron they'd used for this task was clean the heavy layer of soot that was clinging to its surface. It had been impossible to do this without getting some of the thick, black grunge on herself, which was particularly exasperating since she had but the one outfit.

On this day, the clothes in question were in the steaming pot that Stewart had suspended over the fire pit he'd prepared for that purpose. While they soaked, Skye was dressed in her nightgown, covered by the long coat she'd worn throughout the winter.

As she stirred the garments, she thought how lucky the men were to have an extra outfit each, since they'd not been wearing nightclothes when the fire had swept through. She found that she was daydreaming about bolts of cotton in lovely colours and imagined herself sewing stylish new dresses.

Sewing had been one thing her mother was especially good at, and she'd painstakingly taught Skye how to make her stitches smooth and consistent. Skye recalled how, at first, her hand had cramped after holding the needle for any length of time. After a while, she learned to let her hand relax even as she drew the thread through the fabric, and it gave her no further difficulty.

It suddenly struck her that she didn't even know what the latest styles were. Without the general store, there were no sketches to use as a guide in designing their clothes. Goodness knew whether the Carpenters would rebuild the store, and if so, when.

What does that matter, Skye thought, shaking her head and remembering how she once cared about such unimportant things. Now all that mattered was that they were all alive. So many had lost their lives and so many others had been horribly injured.

She leaned forward and fished a shirt out of the bubbling pot. Steam rose from it as she laid it across the scrubbing board that Logan had made for her when it was storming too hard for him to venture from the cellar.

I'll *never* get this clean, she thought, shaking her head at the ingrained soil. Still, she began to rub the shirt along the ribs of the scrubbing board, pushing it back and forth without much hope that her efforts would be successful.

Surprisingly, the soil loosened and, after being dipped into the cauldron and worked on the board several more times it was, if not exactly pristine, much improved from her efforts.

It was slow work, for almost every article of clothing needed the same amount of labour before Skye was satisfied with the results. When she was, she took each item to the line Logan had put up for her and fastened it with the wooden pegs she'd made during the many long hours underground. It had been her first time carving something like that, and the pegs weren't as smooth and uniform as those she'd seen her father make, but they held the clothes just fine and Skye was proud of her handiwork.

It was a perfect day for drying clothes — sunny with a good breeze blowing. The air was a little cool yet, but spring was definitely there. As she worked, Skye drank in the sight of the greens all around her, blades pushing up from the earth, buds bursting out of the trees and bushes.

It was surprising to see which trees were still alive. Some that she'd never have guessed to have the least bit of life in them were greening, while others that seemed quite unharmed remained naked in silhouette against the landscape.

Soon, Skye would be able to gather dandelion greens for a lovely salad — it would be the first bite of anything green they'd had in months. Her mouth watered at the thought.

She was down to the last three pieces of clothing when something caught her eye: a movement to her far right — someone coming along the road.

Happy for an excuse to rest her aching hands, which were raw from the harsh soap and repeated scrubbings, Skye stood and watched as the figure drew nearer. The movements were familiar — the rhythm of the step, the slight move from side to side — but even so, she could almost see the face before she recognized the gait.

"Tavish!" Skye's feet seemed to move on their own before she'd even formed the thought to run to her brother. As she reached him, his face burst into a wide smile.

"You've grown an inch or more," he said, looking her over.

"You can *see*?" she cried, heart pounding.

"Not so well as I once did, but enough to manage,"

he said, tousling her hair. "And it seems a little better all the time."

"Did you receive our message about Uncle William?"

"With many thanks," he said. "Does he mean to stay in Newcastle?"

"For now," Skye told him. "And you? Have you come to stay?"

"You couldn't pay me to go back," he said. "I've been nearly mad waiting for the ice to go out and for someone to ferry me across the river. There's much to be done and it's high time I joined the others."

"I'm glad, though you'll not find it a joy living in the cellar. It's so dark all of the time!"

"I suppose I got used to the dark these past months," Tavish said with a shrug. He was determined not to let Skye see that the thought bothered him. After all, she'd already been living underground for months. He could bear the darkness as well as she. Never mind if it reminded him of the fear and anguish he'd been through when his eyes had shut out the light.

"How are Hannah and the baby?"

"They're fine, though I think Hannah is anxious to be back in a place of her own," he told her, glad that the subject had been changed. "Ellie-Sue doesn't cry so much as she used to, which is a relief on poor Mr. Cullwick's nerves."

"And the others? How are the Chapmans?"

"The Chapmans are both well. Such good people!"

"They truly are," Skye agreed wholeheartedly. "And little Henry Fraser — is he still there?"

"He is, and he's doing fine. His mother came for him at last and took him off, only there was some kind of problem and she had to bring him back. But now she comes every day and spends time with him. She said that she's afraid he'll forget who his own mother is."

"So, Miranda has gotten over her ... illness?" Skye asked, picturing the troubled face of the woman standing on the dock watching for her husband.

"She's very thin, but other than that she seems fine to me," Tavish said, not entirely sure what Skye was asking.

"I mean, she doesn't seem at all off in the head?"

"No more than most women," he said with a teasing smile.

Skye gave him a gentle swat on the arm. "I don't suppose you think that of *Abby Gunn*," she said.

"I must agree that, for a girl, Abby is uncommonly sensible," Tavish told her. He managed a straight face, but his eyes lit up and this gave him away to his sister, who was delighted to see his reaction.

"Oh! I almost forgot! What happened to the little girl you brought with you when you came to Chatham?" she asked. "Little Laura Blake?"

Tavish told her all that had taken place with Laura and how the Chapmans were now raising her as their own. Skye's mouth fell open when she heard of how Mr. Cullwick had intervened and had paid out a large sum of money to save the girl from her callous relatives.

"It hardly seems possible," she told Tavish. "I believed him incapable of thinking of anyone but himself. It must be that seeing so much misfortune had an effect on him."

"It may be that," Tavish said. "But I'm more inclined to think it was seeing the goodness in others that made the difference."

October 7, 1826

Reverend John Webber looked out over the crowd that was gathered before him. He raised a hand and the low murmurs that are always present in a waiting assembly quieted and stopped.

Near the front row, his remaining children — John Junior, Clara, and Martin — stood and watched solemnly. Webber's throat tightened at the thought that they had been without a mother for the difficult year that had just passed. His eyes lingered on them for a moment before lifting and looking slowly over the gathered crowd. He cleared his throat.

"Brothers and Sisters," he began, "we all know what this day signifies. Death and destruction, fear and flight. We have come together to remember a day of loss and heartache.

"It is not to refresh fading memories that we have gathered. Indeed, we are in no danger of forgetting the wreckage that was this place but one short year ago, or the suffering we endured on that day and in the months that followed. Some bore greater losses than others, it is true, but not one among us escaped unharmed.

"And yet, it is with grateful hearts that we gather here today, for we have truly known what it is to be delivered. As David wrote in the 23rd Psalm, we have walked through the valley of the shadow of death. And in that valley we found new faith and hope."

As Reverend Webber spoke, Collin Haverill felt as though the pastor's remarks were meant for him alone. Those first months after the fire had been torture. No matter how hard he tried, he could not rid himself of thoughts of the suffering his wife and sons had endured, or the horror that had been their final moments.

There had been times when he had felt as though he could not go on one minute longer, that his heart would surely explode with grief. But other moments, anger had built in him until he wanted to roar like a beast and rip apart anything in his path with his bare hands.

And then, one night, alone in the ruins of Newcastle, he had fallen to his knees feeling so wholly broken and lost that the only thought his weary mind could form was, "*Why?*" This had become a prayer of sorts, as though he were imploring God for an answer — anything that would make sense of the senselessness of it all.

There had been no answer. At least, not one he had expected. But, in that moment, something poured into him and filled his broken heart with a strange feeling of peace. And Collin had risen to his feet in wonder with a new thought, one so simple and pure that he felt compelled to speak it aloud.

"I don't *need* to know *why*," he murmured, as though repeating words he had been told, "I only need to *trust*."

It has not been an easy road, Collin thought as he drew his thoughts back to what the pastor was saying, but since that day he had known a measure of peace, for in that moment he had learned what it truly meant to trust God.

Next to Collin, Hannah and Logan also reflected on the changes they had known since that terrible night. The fire had taken their home and possessions, but they had come to look on these losses as less than nothing. The security, and even prosperity, that had once seemed so important paled in comparison to the sufferings of those who had buried loved ones.

The only thing that truly mattered was that their children had been spared. All else could be rebuilt and replaced.

Holding little Elizabet Susan, Hannah thought how significant it was that this was their daughter's birthday. A reminder that, even amidst death and destruction, new life had come.

Of the Haverills that were assembled there that day, Tavish was the least inclined to thoughts of what they had all been through. From the moment he had realized that his world had turned dark, he had begun to learn how to live in the moment, and this had become a habit that would stay with him.

No longer would he fret over what was or might be. The months that he had spent with little or no vision had taught him that sight comes from more than just the eyes, and this understanding would serve him well through his whole life.

Stewart Drummond shifted impatiently as Reverend Webber invited the members of the crowd to raise their voices together in a hymn of praise. Hannah sometimes worried that the boy had too much restlessness in him and, though Stewart clearly had a good heart, it was often difficult to pin him down to do the things he ought to be doing. She needn't have worried. Stewart had been greatly drawn to the steady stream of vessels that had made their way to the Miramichi with goods for the impoverished. He had spent many hours aboard them talking to the crews and helping to carry out supplies. During one such event Stewart realized that he too was meant for a sailor's life.

William English listened thoughtfully as Pastor Webber delivered the message. At the same time, he looked forward to the day when he also might offer words of hope and comfort.

Remembering the desperation and despair he'd felt when she was leaving, William was surprised at how calmly he'd received Charlott Willoughby's reply to the letter he'd sent, telling her of his plans to become a minister. She'd made it clear that, while she might be willing to step into a lower station than she'd been born into, there was no way she was going to be a preacher's wife. Added, almost as an afterthought, was the declaration that she had, after all, decided to remain in England for another year.

Even so, William felt content that whatever might lie ahead, there was nothing that he need fear or regret.

At her stepmother's side, Skye Haverill felt the weight of the solemn anniversary in ways she had never expected. So much had happened since the terrible night of the fire!

All around her, she saw friends and classmates, neighbours and families clustered together. Their faces showed so many things, and Skye felt as though each feeling reflected in the expressions around her were rising up from her own heart.

Sorrow. Helplessness. Weariness. Determination. Hope. Faith. Patience. Courage. Thankfulness.

It was all there, jumbled into the past year, preserved in them as hardships overcome, lessons learned, and blessings received.

The towns were rising again, with many homes already rebuilt. Putting broken families and shattered lives back together would take a little longer, but the healing had begun.

They had been through so much, and had survived. But they had not done it alone. From across the river and the province, from across the country and other countries, hands and hearts had reached out.

These thoughts overwhelmed her and tears fell, running down Skye's cheeks. She brushed them away and managed a tremulous smile as she felt Hannah's hand, gentle but strong, on her shoulder.

AUTHOR'S NOTE

*W*hen I first learned of the Great Fire of Miramichi and determined to write this story, I believed it would chiefly be a tale of tragedy and devastation. Very early into my research, I realized how wrong that assumption had been.

The Miramichi Fire took lives. (Among them, a number of my ancestors.) By the time it had run its deadly course, it had burned one fifth of the province — more than three million acres of land. It destroyed buildings, possessions, livestock, and provisions. It left many facing the winter ahead both homeless and impoverished.

Despite that, this story is ultimately one of triumph. For as word of the tragedy spread, the response, both from the public and from various governments, was overwhelming.

Below is a summary of a few of the events, driven by the kindness and generosity of strangers, that enabled the survival of entire communities.

On the 15th day of October, the messengers who had been dispatched to Fredericton, New Brunswick, and Halifax, Nova Scotia reached their destinations.

It would have touched the hearts of those left destitute if they had seen firsthand the compassion with which news of their plight was received, or if they had known what actions and efforts would be made to assist and support them in their time of need.

When news of the calamity reached His Excellency, Sir Howard Douglas, Lieutenant-Governor of New Brunswick in Fredericton, he lost no time in responding to the tale of tragedy and hardship. Douglas called for a council that very day, and the council swiftly passed a resolution to send a messenger on to Quebec, where he was to purchase 1,000 barrels of flour, 500 barrels of pork, and an assortment of clothing, up to a value of £6,000.

When the council had completed its work and done all that was within its power, Sir Douglas called for a public meeting, where he addressed the people.

Although Fredericton itself had also known devastation from the fire, its losses did not compare to those of the towns along the Miramichi River and other smaller settlements in the province. Still, Sir Douglas gave full consideration to the difficulties being faced locally before outlining what had been done for the immediate relief and assistance of the people of Miramichi. He then appealed to those in attendance to start a general fund that could be applied not only for the urgent needs, but also toward the enormous job of rebuilding the destroyed towns.

In spite of their own losses, the people of Fredericton responded with great generosity. A committee that was already in place to raise funds for the damages at Fredericton swiftly concluded that the need at Miramichi surpassed that of their own townsmen, and £250 of the money they had raised was remitted to that end.

Sir Douglas had already made a significant contribution from his own funds at the council meeting, but he pledged a further donation to the public fund. He then closed his address to the people and set out for the Miramichi.

Douglas felt it was his duty to go to the scene of devastation in order to provide what support he was able to offer. As well, he was determined to see for himself that enough had been done to ensure the immediate survival of the sufferers before winter arrived and added to the devastation that had already occurred.

The city of Saint John had been spared from the fire. Its inhabitants also responded swiftly and in very short order had sent off two vessels loaded with provisions and clothing of all kinds.

Countless smaller New Brunswick communities also sent aid.

When news of the fire arrived in Halifax, those who heard it were greatly moved by the suffering of their neighbouring colony.

Recognizing the gravity of the situation, and the need for immediate action, they arranged to have hand-bills printed and circulated throughout the town. A meeting was scheduled at the County Court House for 9:00 the very next morning.

The meeting began with donations in the amount of £1,200 pouring in from those in attendance. Committees were sent out to collect further subscriptions through-out the town and peninsula.

Discussions followed as to what further measures were within their power to carry out for the aid of those who had been left destitute.

A plan of action was quickly put in place and a rider was sent overland to the people of Miramichi that very day. His responsibility was to take word of what was be-ing done so that the victims of the fire might be encour-aged by news that help would soon be on the way.

On Monday, October 17, His Excellency, Sir James Kempt, the Lieutenant-Governor of Nova Scotia, con-vened the Legislative and Executive Council to deter-mine what could be done on that level.

Sir Kempt was pleased to advise the council that Rear Admiral Lake, the Commander in Chief of His Majesty's ships on that station, had kindly offered to send HMS *Orestes* to Miramichi to carry provisions to that unhappy location. The Nova Scotian council agreed that the cir-cumstances called for every possible effort to provide help and relief to their sister colony. A second committee was formed, with instructions to work together with the committee formed the day before at the public meeting.

The two groups worked together securing food, clothing, bedding, and medicines as well as medical attendance for the wounded. Volunteers worked diligently at the task of gathering provisions and getting them onto the vessels that would carry them to the Miramichi. So extraordinary were their efforts that the following Tuesday HMS *Orestes*, along with the schooners *Active*, *Albion*, and *Elizabet* sailed for Miramichi loaded with food, clothing, and other provisions.

The *Orestes* was captained by Commander Henry Litchfield, who took himself from a sickbed in order to help his fellow man.

Although Halifax itself was just recovering from a long depression, its good people had done all that they could possibly do to help their fellow man. In examples of generosity, the garrison and the navy in harbour gave a day's pay, church collections were sent in, and it was reported that servants requested that their employers settle their wages so that they could add their modest contributions to the cause. Before long, the subscriptions from that city alone reached £2,000.

All through Nova Scotia, Halifax's example was followed. Cash and provisions were gathered in many communities and over the next few weeks a number of additional vessels loaded with emergency supplies set sail for New Brunswick.

Newfoundland, Prince Edward Island, and Quebec responded in like manner, collecting subscriptions, obtaining provisions, and sending them as immediately as possible to the scene of devastation and misery.

South of the border, Americans added their efforts in those places where news of the tragedy made its way. New York, Boston, and Eastport were among those who gathered thousands of dollars in donations for their northern neighbours.

Distribution of Goods:

Every man, woman, and child was given one warm suit of clothes and a pair of shoes. Other items were given out on the basis of family size. For example, a family of six would receive, in addition to the shoes and clothing, twenty-four yards of osnaburgh,* four blankets, a barrel of flour, one barrel of meal and one of pork (or two barrels of fish), six barrels of potatoes, and a quantity of tea and sugar.

The total losses of property, possessions, and livestock of the Great Miramichi Fire were estimated at just

---

* Coarse, brown linen.

over £200,000, of which very little was insured.

The loss of life, with more than 160 dead, was im-measurable.

ACKNOWLEDGEMENTS

The author gratefully acknowledges the support of The New Brunswick Arts Board.

Very sincere thanks to Alan MacEachern (Department of History, University of Western Ontario), who generously pointed me toward the resources he had uncovered in his own research on the subject of the Great Fire of Miramichi. Alan MacEachern's factual account of the fire is slated for publication in 2008.

Thanks also to Marsha Skrypuch for graciously sharing her expertise on historical fiction and to the following Kidcrit members who offered feedback on several chapters: Helaine Becker, kc dyer, Alison Flensburg, Carolyn Gray, Natalie Hyde, Sharon Jones, Paulette MacQuarr, and Martha Martin.

As always, I am grateful for continuing support and encouragement from:

My husband, partner, and best friend, Brent. Love never fails.

My parents, Bob and Pauline Russell.

My son Anthony, his wife Maria, and daughters Emilee and Ericka. My daughter Pamela and her husband, David Jardine. My brothers and their families: Danny and Gail; Andrew, Shelley, and Bryce. My "other" family: Ron and Phoebe Sherrard, Ron Sherrard and Dr. Kiran Pure, Bruce and Roxanne Mullin, and Karen Sherrard.

Friends: Janet Aube, Jimmy Allain, Karen Arseneault, Dawn Black, Angi Garofolo, Karen Gauvin, John Hambrook, Sandra Henderson, Jim Hennessy, Mary Matchett, Johnnye Montgomery, Mark Rhodes, Linda Stevens, Pam Sturgeon, Paul Theriault, and Bonnie Thompson.

My sixth-grade teacher, Alf Lower, for his continuing support and encouragement and for his friendship.

At The Dundurn Group, the whole team and particularly my editor, Barry Jowett, for his excellent direction with this story, and for occasionally answering my e-mails.

Readers! Hearing from you is the *best* part of writing, and I love getting your letters and e-mails. Special thanks to Hasan Aydar, Alaura Campbell, Chelsea Derry, Young Lark Jin, Jordan Kidney, Marley Kingston, Sarah Koziol, Julia MacDonald, Meg MacDonald, Kieran MacNamara, Samantha Mason, Melissa Murdock,

Monica Richard, Jorden Rutter, Candace Sherrard and Mallory Watling.

Remember the tears and toil that built our world.